in an attic from which she can see a sliver of the moor. As well as novels for teenagers, she writes for adults and *Flames* (Virago) was awarded a prize.

Between books, she has held writing residences and she does workshops and readings.

She enjoys theatre, film, conversation, walking in the Dales and studying any subject that takes her fancy. But she is never really satisfied unless she is working on a book, preferably very different from the previous one.

Praise for June Oldham

'The haunting strangeness of the setting, the power of Oldham's language and imagery, and the emotional immediacy of the characters' situation will remain indelibly in readers' memories.' *Booklist*

'June Oldham deploys her impressive powers of description and insightful portrayal of character in another highly-charged story about revelation and twisted relationships . . . Oldham is a thrilling writer.' *TES*

Also by June Oldham

Escape
Smoke Trail
The Raven Waits
Undercurrents
Foundling

Other titles published by Hodder Children's Books

Dead Negative
Control-Shift
Seed Time
Nick Manns

Heathrow Nights
Jan Mark

Light
Alan Davidson

Sea Hawk, Sea Moon
Beverley Birch

Blackthorn, Whitethorn
The Flight of the Emu
THE MOVING TIMES TRILOGY:
Bloom of Youth
Grandmother's Footsteps
Stronger than Mountains
Rachel Anderson

Shadow of the Beast
Owl Light
Dark of the Moon
Maggie Pearson

In the
Blood

June Oldham

*Hodder
Children's
Books*

A division of Hodder Headline Limited

For Margery Bullock

One

Rigby opened the curtains of his bedroom and squinted through the mid-morning sun. It had found the cherry tree and was brushing over its leaves, polishing their yellow; those of a maple it stained a deeper mahogany. Occasionally, in a leisurely fashion, a leaf left its branch and dropped into the mist still crawling round the mossed spokes of roots.

'You could start raking up,' his father had said. 'It's never too early.' That was typical of his father; he enjoyed making a job spin out, taking twice as long as was necessary. Rigby did not object to raking, but not piecemeal; he would wait until the very last leaf was shed.

He heard the garage doors open, an engine turn over. From the hallway there were calls, goodbyes, references to shopping, something about a dress: his mother and sister, dedicated to conscientious occupation. He went downstairs and opened the refrigerator, though with little hope. It was in its usual Friday condition. He tapped a bare shelf to test the echo, then made himself a mug of instant coffee, drank it at the back door and studied the mist from this lower angle. Wondering whether he was becoming mist-fixated, he returned to his room, chose a CD, plugged in his head phones and stretched on his bed.

The mattress sloped under him as someone sat on its edge. A finger poked his thigh. Rigby opened his eyes and watched Carol mouth a paragraph or two. Then he uncovered his ears.

'So I'm worried,' she concluded.

He frowned and nodded slowly, simulated sympathy.

'Would you go?'

'I'm busy.' If he had asked, 'Where to?' he would have indicated a flicker of interest. That was not advisable.

'He's not answering the phone.'

The situation became clearer. 'Perhaps he's just gone out. For a walk.'

'Grandpa doesn't know how to.'

'He can find his way to the pub.'

'It isn't open yet.'

Rigby glanced at his watch. 'Soon will be.'

'I've been dialling for the last half hour, every three minutes.' Carol won a lot of compliments for persistence. Rigby did not envy her. 'Either he's not there, or he isn't answering.'

'Full marks.'

'You know what happened the last time.'

He nodded. Their mother had informed the police and they had hunted Gilbert down, helicopters thundering, throbbing low over moors and valleys.

Carol demanded, 'And what was the end of it?'

'They found him.'

'He was stuck in a psychiatric ward for three months. That's how it ended.'

'He didn't seem to mind. "I adore these psychologists," he said. "Especially the female variety."'

'At his age!' Carol was briefly distracted from her purpose. 'He told me, "They're very interested in my colourful life."'

'I suppose you could claim grey is a colour.'

'Won't you look in, Rig?' Now it was 'look in', a casual visit conveniently en route to somewhere else, not a pull up switchback gradients. Carol's resemblance to their mother depressed him.

'Why don't you?'

'I have to go into school.'

'When it's closed?' There was staff training, hence the holiday.

3

'We're having a rehearsal for the choir concert. Mr Beddoes is giving up his lunch hour.'

Ignoring the man's sacrifice, Rigby argued, 'You've still time.'

'Rig, I've already cycled to Grandfather's once this morning.'

'Why was that?'

'Because I wanted him to see this. Have you really, really not noticed?' She stood up and twirled round, showing off her dress. 'It's on loan from the Playhouse wardrobe.'

'Who would want to *hire* that?'

'I could have had a Flapper's dress, or a Shakespearean, or a Restoration serving wench only Mrs Hickson thought this suited my type. Very nineteen forties. I mean, it's Utility. They had to have coupons.'

'Then they were robbed.'

Seeing his eyes had shifted to her hair rolled in a tube round her head and the three vicious metal curlers furling her fringe, Carol explained, 'I'm practising. Mrs Hickson suggested a uniform for you. I brought one so you could try it on. That would make a sort of family theme.' When he had woken up that morning the battle dress, gaiters and forage cap were laid out like grave cerements beside him. They were now a heap of khaki on the floor.

'How many times do I have to tell you, Carol? If I go to Heather Dale's party, and I haven't accepted yet, I am not – watch my lips – *not* turning up in fancy dress.'

'But Heather is set on it. Why must you be so awkward?'

'It's a question of keeping my options open. And if you want my honest opinion, you'd look better if you went in your . . .' He halted, unable to recall a single garment in Carol's limitless wardrobe.

'Grandpa liked it, anyway. I'm sorry, now, that he did.' She paused. 'That's why I was ringing him when I got home. I shouldn't have done it, Rigby. I shouldn't have gone in the dress to show him. I didn't think. Seeing it . . . he was upset. He was alright at first. He put on one of his records and he taught me the fox trot: slow, slow, quick quick, slow. Like he had danced it. He said I could be mistaken for Gran. Then he said, "Excuse me, my dear. Fancy me dancing without smartening up!" and he took the needle off the record and started rummaging in a cupboard. I asked him if he had mislaid something and he said it was lost, really, so there was no sense in looking. As soon as I got home, I tried to call him. I thought if I could keep him talking, the mood would pass over and he'd be back to his usual self.'

Rigby would have been prepared to chance his grandfather's not returning to that; another sort of self might be preferable. But he kept quiet; Carol was more fond of Gilbert than he was. Because of this, he told her, 'I suppose I'd better get my bike out.' He slipped his head phones over his ears, savoured a few beats, and switched off.

'Thanks, Rig.'

'Any suggestions on procedure if he's not at home?'

Carol shook her head.

'Oh, come on! It's too early to get worked up.' He thought, Fancy it getting to her like this; she's convinced it is serious.

'It's my fault. Reminding him of Gran. That's what Mum said it was all about, last time.'

'Ben thought it was more complicated. He said if anyone could pull the wool over psychologists' eyes, it was Grandad.'

She flared, 'What else could it be? Ben's a know-all.'

'So he was right?'

Carol answered, 'Don't forget your mobile,' and sieved through the sedimentary strata on the floor.

A mobile phone had been an alpha toy in the first months but it had one massive snag: people abused it. No matter where you were or what you were doing, people could get in touch. There would be requests such as: 'Would you please call at the butcher's for the meat?' and 'Mr Hobhouse would be grateful if you would pick up his prescription,' – and next door's repaired washing machine, and Auntie's cobra from the vet. Worse, there would be unsubtle threats: 'I'm wondering whether you'll be staying for tea at Tim's,' or reports to keep you up to date with global events: 'I thought I should let you know that I've missed the train but will be on the next.' Therefore, when Carol handed him the phone and cautioned him to keep it switched on, Rigby answered, 'I'll think about it.'

'Keeping your options open?'

'Something like that.' Another way of putting it was: a mobile phone is the technological equivalent of being tied to your mother's apron strings.

The state of the kitchen suggested that the local supermarket had been re-located, but his mother had been excused the overall and cap. She looked content, filling the shelves. He investigated the bags and removed a bar of chocolate.

'You'll spoil your appetite,' Daphne objected.

'I'll take the risk.'

'Lunch will be ready very soon.' This claim was against all evidence.

'I shan't be long.'

'Where are you going?'

'Out. To take the air. Fit in a spot of exercise.'

'It's still quite soggy under foot.'

'I'll be on my bicycle.'

'Strong winds are forecast.'

'I'm more bothered about the flood warnings, Mother.'

'Flood warnings? I haven't heard . . .' She stopped, thought, was touched by a revelation, and gave a tentative smile.

Something on his cycle clicked as he wheeled it out of the garage but he did not stop to investigate, wanting to get the chore over. Hungry, he wondered what his mother intended for lunch.

He lived at the edge of the town among houses built on former meadows. So he had hardly settled into a smooth cycling rhythm before he had left the Avenues, the Crescents, the Groves, the Drives and was riding between hedges. On the survey maps, the road was coloured yellow which denoted a width of less than four metres. Rigby traced it in his head.

It climbed up contour lines, curved round hills to take ways that horses and carts had found easier; it straightened for a length where a path had once skirted the headland of strip fields, or it ran in the shade of a wood; and all the time it remained close to the sinuous river.

Rigby was fascinated by maps, how they translated the land, offered you the lanes and tracks over it, showed you the relationship of its features that your eye could not reach. And they revealed all the smaller details: ruins, shippons, unsuspected hollows, abandoned buildings that you would not otherwise come across except by chance. Wherever he visited, he always returned to study it on the map.

The lane dipped and he free-wheeled until he came to a farm, rode through the gate and left his cycle against the wall of a shed. Nearby, a long belt of trees indicated the course of a beck. Taking the path that ran beside it, Rigby was not long in reaching his grandfather's house.

Two

The house stood in a natural amphitheatre formed by a crescent of trees. Further along, meadows took over and there was a small collection of houses, but despite their proximity, this one was solitary; it seemed to be cut off. Visitors with cars came by the road, unseen but not far away, then they trudged down the path, grumbling about the mud when they were too lightly shod.

Disdaining the plank bridging the beck, Rigby waded across. He squeezed water from his jeans, emptied his trainers and strode through the margin of roughly scythed grass, a lawn according to his mother. In the porch, propped against logs, was a spade tipped with dried earth; a cycle cape hung from a hook. Rigby tapped on the door and shouted, 'Grandfather!' and 'Is anyone at home?' There was no answer.

Presumably his grandfather had gone out; he might at that moment be sitting in the bar of The Grand Old

Duke of York. Rigby felt stupid; he had let himself be persuaded into a wild goose chase, and he composed a few annihilating sentences for Carol.

It was very quiet. The beck's ripple was faint; the birds were mute. The house was folded into itself, its curtains closed; its shadow, cast by the light struggling through branches, was stunted and dank. He shouted again, 'Grandfather!' and rattled the knob. The door gave, opened at his push.

The living room was empty, and the kitchen. Panicked by pictures of his grandfather ill, dying, Rigby rushed upstairs. But everything was normal: Gilbert's bed was unmade, a discarded shirt hung over the wardrobe door, in a saucer cigarette butts lay on a pyre of ash, in the spare bedroom a carton of apples stood on the bare mattress, a pair of stiff socks hung over the bath, and the lavatory remained proof against the scented sprays introduced by Rigby's mother. In comparison, the living room was unnatural, Rigby thought. All that could be judged as untidy was the fireplace heaped with cinders and the scorched remnants of logs. He looked through the kitchen window and saw that his grandfather was not asleep on the bench below it. He thought: I may as well search round a bit while I'm here.

A glance at the clock by the hearth told him that he

had done the journey in record time. So Carol wouldn't have left yet for her choir practice. I'll let her know the score, he thought. At the telephone, dialling home, he noted that there was no fault on the line.

'I've been wondering where you are,' his mother answered and repeated the formula, 'I'm about to prepare some lunch.'

'Don't worry, Mum. I'm at Grandfather's.'

'I see. Give him my love, won't you?'

'Mum, do you mind fetching Carol? I'd like a word.'

'She's gone.'

'Already?'

'She left about half an hour ago, I'm afraid. Shall I give her a message?'

'Please.' He paused to work it out. 'Would you just tell her that she was right.'

'Right?'

'Yes. About something she was thinking – suspected. I didn't agree with her. Could you let her know that now I do?'

'Oh, Rigby, I'm so glad you can say that. I mean, admit you made a mistake. So few people can; they think it's a sign of weakness. When, in truth, it's a very mature thing.' At present, Daphne was experimenting with 'mature', a description that Rigby had decided was less an attempt at compliment than, more sinister, a form of brain-washing. Two months earlier, she had been obsessed with 'aggressive'. He was not entirely happy with the substitution.

As lingeringly Daphne said good bye, overjoyed that at last her precepts and example were encouraging some modest buds, Rigby considered the fact of Carol's early leaving. He looked at his watch. It showed one o'clock. For a moment he was disorientated, as if he had leapt an hour, then he slid back to midday and again he regarded the hands of the case clock.

He disliked its name: grandfather clock. Gilbert would say to him, 'That's yours when I'm gone,' and Rigby could find no way of declining it, a great clumsy thing, the oak case carved with scrolls, the door inlaid with brass, the top castellated. It was a fort of a clock. 'Lovely action,' Gilbert would assure him, sensible of Rigby's lack of enthusiasm. 'Eight day movement.' But today the hands on the enamelled face had stopped. Investigating, Rigby opened the tall door. Packages had been stuffed in the case, stopping the pendulum. Released, they fell at his feet.

As he placed them on the table, documents poked out of a card wallet, the contents of a bag rattled, the corner of another split showing a bundle of letters. The stamps on them were blue, bearing the profile of a clean-shaven monarch and the price was 2½d; the envelopes that he could see were addressed to Miss F. Kilshaw. This was his grandmother's maiden name and seemed to confirm Carol's reason for Gilbert's flight. That must have happened after midday; it was then that Gilbert had put the packages in the case and so stopped the clock. This meant that while Carol was ringing, every three minutes, he was at home occupied in rummaging and determined to repulse contact. After that, he had put this cache out of sight.

Taken by cold, Rigby chose to blame his soaked denims. He switched on the electric fire and stood close. First he would go to The Duke of York, following the path by the beck as his grandfather would, through the cluster of houses and along the primary road. If Gilbert were not there, what then?

Contemplating his question, he looked across at the packages. Among them was a slim rectangle, buff coloured, a stiff wad of pleats. Impatient, Rigby waited until his jeans were satisfactorily roasted, switched off the fire, picked up his find and without thought, automatically because what he held was a map, he pushed it into a pocket. Then, his legs smarting, lagged in a mist of steam, he left the house.

There were few customers in The Grand Old Duke of York. Even so, at the sight of Rigby, the landlord pointed to the notice prohibiting under-age sales.

'I'm not trying to buy a drink,' Rigby told him.

'That's just as well.'

'I was wondering whether my grandfather is here.'

The landlord gestured to three men playing dominoes at a table and a couple roosting on stools at the bar.

'Has he been in?'

'Not since last Tuesday.'

The man on the stool explained that Gilbert 'liked a good quiz.'

'That's all he comes for. He'll sit here all night over half a glass of bitter,' the landlord remarked, resentful at such meagre business.

'He fancies the company, Walt,' the man argued, conciliatory. 'You keep a tight house.'

His companion asked, 'Why would you be looking for Gilbert, Sunshine?'

'Don't you be nosey,' the man rebuked.

'It's not a state secret, is it?' she addressed Rigby. 'Here, would you like this basket of chips? They came with the sandwiches. I haven't touched them. Untouched by human hands, unless you include his lordship in that category.' She nodded towards the landlord.

Rigby had the information he needed. To stay risked further questions, but hunger won. 'Thanks,' he said, and started on the chips.

'They'll put you on nicely,' the man assured him.

'So you're grandson to Gilbert,' the woman stated.

'One of them.'

'And I know which. You're the copper nob.'

The man laughed.

Rigby looked at the chips and calculated that it would take two minutes to finish them. He answered, 'Grandfather calls me that, now and again.'

'Well, I'm not sure I would, exactly. Copper doesn't do it justice, if you understand me. It's softer and it's got a deeper hue. Stan, what's your opinion?' she appealed to her husband.

Rigby relinquished the last mouthful of chips. 'Thanks,' he said, handing back the basket.

Concentrating, she leant closer and squinted as if examining paint samples. 'It depends how the light falls, doesn't it? Just now there's a hint of red cabbage but a minute before it was nearer mahogany.'

Incensed, he snapped, 'Are you sure it isn't greengage?' Striding to the door, he heard the woman's voice following him, 'And he's got the temper to match!'

The man called, 'I'll have a word to say to your grandfather.'

Rigby turned, answered, harsh, 'You'll have to find him first.'

People were forever accusing him of temper, blaming

16

it on the colour of his hair. He wished they could be more imaginative, not so predictable. They never said: 'With that hair he can't be asked to weed the garden, or get up at dawn, turn down his music, fumigate his bedroom.' And another thing, he went on, you stand out, you're immediately distinguishable. The report would come in: 'Some boys were creating a din on the bus/seen messing about in the physics lab/found stacked in a kiosk/skateboarding in the golf club car park. No precise names are available, but one young man had a mop of flaming hair.' The only chance he had of merging with the crowd was to encase the stuff in his school cap, but since to wear that was a rule, he rarely did.

By this time The Duke of York was well behind him. Recalled to his reason for trudging beside a primary road in the draught of fast vehicles, he said to himself, furious again, It's just like Grandfather to mention my hair. He has a fixation about it. Only a few days earlier he had said, 'I bet anyone looking for a fight thinks twice at the sight of that thatch.' Annoyed that Gilbert had presumed to comment on it, he had retorted, 'You're wrong, Grandfather. The bruisers in my year are colour blind,' and the other's eyes had swerved away.

By the side of the road there was a highways sign picturing a cow determinedly plodding, a caution to traffic that cattle might cross. Leaning against it was a board on which was painted: Latest score, Cows – 5, Cars – 0. Rigby laid the board on the damp grass and sat down, about to consider where to look next, when he heard an engine decelerate and Ben drew up.

'Hi, there,' he greeted. 'Like a lift?'

'I'm not sure.'

'Waiting for someone?'

'No. Inspiration.'

Ben got out of the car. 'Tell your big bro all about it.'

Rigby explained.

'I'm pretty certain he'll have gone off,' Ben said. 'I suppose Mum and Dad ought to be told, but I agree that's not essential at the moment. Don't worry, I'll take the flak. You and Carol won't be blamed.'

'I don't mind if I am.'

'No, but, all the same ... The trouble is, Rigby, you're on your own on this one. All I can do is make a few phone calls, see if Gilbert's in any of the hostels around, but I can't manage any more. Nightingale's working through, soothing fevered brows, so I'm left in charge of George until late tomorrow.'

'Where is he?'

'In the car. It's his favourite place for a snooze. Never fails.'

Rigby got up and peered through the window. Strapped into his seat, his head resting on a cushion, George bubbled peacefully.

'I'm sorry, Rig. I've been taking it that you've decided to carry on looking for Grandfather.'

'I might as well.'

'You can pull out any time.'

'I suppose so. I'll have to think of something to tell Mother.'

'I'll give her a ring, say you're with us and sleeping over.'

'Thanks.'

'I don't think Grandfather will be very far away. Last time he was in the quarry near Dib Bank and the helicopter spotted him when he broke cover.'

'I could look there.'

'It would be a start. I expect he has some favourite hideouts. The quarry could be one. If you like I can make a crafty detour and drop you off at the bottom of Dib Lane.'

It was a short walk down the track to the quarry that a century and a half earlier had provided the building material for nearby farms. Rigby scrambled through shrubs and stood on the quarry's floor. It dipped shallow as a saucer within the walls of hewn rock. Here and there a sapling, unnourished and frail, clung to a shallow ledge but it shaded no niche to hide in. On the ground, the rushes that spiked through pools, the clumps of bilberry, were too low and the sprouts of birch too thin to offer thorough concealment. Once there had been a shed, now it was a heap of planks. Beside it stubs of blackened wood lay in a damp paste of ashes. This hearth was ancient but it was the only sign that any traveller had been there.

Years ago, Rigby might have considered this a good place to play, secluded, safe from supervision; but today, affected by his purpose, he felt disquiet. Except where the track entered, there was no vista. The rim of high wall extended, its lip like a parapet making a hard line between the rock and sky. Above, the afternoon light was tall, limitless; below, it was confined, already dusk. He was not surprised that Gilbert, satisfied at first with the quarry's modest concealment, had finally rushed out and given himself up.

He pushed back to the track, deciding that it was too late to look further, that he would return to the job tomorrow, work out a strategy. This evening he would spend with Ben, take a shift amusing George. But, entering the main road, he was still two miles from his cycle and he resented the distance, grumbling to himself, dispirited and hungry. His thoughts locked on the final, discarded chips.

He had covered temperature and texture and was moving on to taste when he became aware of shouts and his name brokenly whinnied. Recognising the voice, Rigby quickened his pace, then halted. Perhaps the boy behind him had news of Gilbert.

'What is it?' he called.

The other caught up with him, made much of checking his identity in the low light and greeted, 'Mr Livingstone, I presume?'

'You've been looking for me, Stanley?'

'No. I just saw you.'

'Have you seen anyone else?'

'It's only a few minutes since my dad dropped me off.'

'Fair enough. See you, then.'

He resumed walking, but Watkins did not take the hint. He stayed by Rigby's side and reported, 'There was someone with a dog.'

'I'm not interested in anyone with a dog.'

'I don't blame you. I'm not fond of dogs myself.'

It was the sort of crass comment you expected from Watkins, sliding away from the point, suggesting that Rigby was interested in meeting anyone at all, provided he had no dog. Particularly Watkins. He wondered whether it was the other's technique for keeping up the conversation.

Watkins added, 'This dog would have gone for me if the owner hadn't held it off. It should have been muzzled.'

'I don't suppose you advised that.'

'I certainly did not!'

'Wise man.'

A car came towards them, head lights on full beam. Watkins dropped behind, scurried back when the car had gone, and went through the procedure on the advance of a lorry. 'You can certainly walk, Cade,' he puffed.

'I'm in a hurry.'

'Don't think I'm complaining,' Watkins said quickly.

'I didn't think anything.'

'I'll make better time.'

'What do you mean by that?'

'I told you – my dad dropped me off outside The Grand Old Duke of York.'

'He abandoned you, did he?'

They had come to the lane that led to the beck. Rigby turned into it. Watkins followed.

'Dad drove home. He'll be there by now, waiting.'

'Does your family go in much for this sort of thing? I mean, does your father make a habit of dropping you five or six miles from your place so he can have the pleasure of sitting with his feet up, waiting till you get back?'

'He won't have his feet up. He'll be doing his evening routine.'

'Are you sure that's not elbow raising in The Duke?'

Watkins was shocked. 'My father doesn't drink! He has his health to consider.'

Rigby apologised, implausibly.

'He keeps up his exercises.'

'I'm pleased to hear that.'

'But he still gives a lot of thought to mine.'

'What exactly is your father training you for?'

Receiving no answer, Rigby turned his head, but the other's expression was masked by the deepening dusk. He was abruptly contrite, reminded of the feeling that his grandfather sometimes provoked in him. He said, 'Forget it, Watkins. Just joking.'

They had reached the bridge over the beck. Off the lane, lights chequered the windows of the farm; near it was the shed where he had left his bicycle. Rigby told him, 'It's goodbye now. My bike's parked here.'

'You didn't say.'

'Why should I?'

'I mean, I thought you were walking. Walking back home. I told you, the rate you were going, I'd make good time.'

'You said it, not me.'

'Not good time. Better. Much better, Rigby.' He was pleading.

'I can't help that.'

'Half an hour. He said I ought to be able to do it in half an hour.'

'That's impossible.'

'He has very high standards.'

'They've shot right off the scale.'

'Dad might have said three-quarters.'

'Make your mind up.'

'I still can't manage it.'

'You might if you ran.'

'Do you think? Look, if you did the first couple of miles, paced me . . .'

'What?'

'Riding on your bike. I could run alongside.'

'Don't be stupid!'

'It would help.' Watkins' voice had risen.

'I'm not going home. I'm cycling to my brother's.'

'Dad will be standing at the door with his stop watch.'

'You said he'd be doing his routine.'

'He is through that in thirty minutes.'

'In that case, get on with it. While you've been standing here talking you could have trotted half a mile.'

'I'm puffed out.' But Watkins stepped away, walked a few paces, waved, and began to run, making a brave show.

Rigby watched him until he was absorbed into the silent shadows: Watkins the whiner, the hanger-on, show-off, boot-licker, given to bouts of shrill malice, occasionally the form's permitted clown. Then he went through the farm gate and past the shed, not wishing to examine why he was ignoring his cycle, why he had changed his plan, telling himself that it was sensible to find out whether Gilbert had returned to his house. But along the path by the beck his vision was taken by pictures of a figure, stooped, lonely, feeling his way along hedges, his only companion the shackling dark.

When he reached the house, it was unlit and the door remained unlocked.

Three

Someone had entered the house. Rigby knew as soon as he was inside. The packages had been emptied, their contents scattered over the table.

He went into the kitchen. In the tea caddy that doubled as a safe, he found Gilbert's pension book together with £45, mainly in notes. Crammed into the toast rack that served as a filing cabinet, a packet that had held lettuce seeds now stored his grandfather's best watch; another, his prescription for spectacles; next to it his cheque book was folded inside a slim box now empty of throat lozenges. 'I don't know what makes you think burglars wouldn't rifle this lot; they aren't stupid, Grandfather,' he had once upbraided. 'Who's saying anything about burglars?' Gilbert had defended. 'These are where I shan't forget. Your memory plays tricks when you're my age.'

Looking round, Rigby could discern no damage; there was nothing to indicate a thief. Yet Gilbert's most personal belongings had been raked over. Documents fanned out of their card wallet: an insurance policy, an NHS medical card, driving licence, MOT test certificate, receipts of bills, all the forms that officially confirmed Gilbert's existence. Coins, discoloured, their value stamped in centimes, were among buckles, a Regimental cap badge, a penknife, a piece of khaki fabric worked with a single stripe. Letters bulged from their bond of grubby ribbon.

Rigby tried to remember how everything had looked when he had stood drying his jeans. Grouping the items together, slotting them into the place they had occupied, he found that one was missing, the map. He pulled it out of his pocket, realising that this was the target of the hunt. The intruder must have been Gilbert himself.

He stroked a finger down the map's cover, smoothed out a bent corner. It was odd that his grandfather should possess this. He never ventured further than fifty or so miles from home, not because he was ill or frail but because he was not interested. He would answer an invitation with: 'I've done my travelling.' By this, he meant in the army. This reason annoyed Rigby; he thought it self-righteous and smug. But then his grandfather's face would twitch.

He opened the map and balanced it on top of the clutter, but before he could examine it, the telephone rang. Rigby waited until it stopped, dialled 1471, found the caller was Ben, and dialled his number.

'Sorry about that,' he said. He could hear George in full voice. 'I thought it might be Carol or Mother.'

'They think you are here. Why aren't you?'

'I decided to check whether he had come back.'

'He hasn't taken his car.' It was kept in a garage among the houses further up the beck. 'After I'd dropped you, I had a look. Hang on a minute.' Then his voice soothed, 'Now young feller, take it easy, else you'll rupture yourself. Let's go for a stroll.' The wheels of a buggy squeaked and the cries diminished; a damp retching entered the handset.

'I'd forgotten about the car,' Rigby said. So why had his grandfather wanted a map? 'Ben, he's been home. A lot of his stuff is messed up.'

'Sure it wasn't a burglar?'

'Yes.'

The wails were resumed. Above them, Ben confided, 'I don't know whether this is hunger or wind. I think I ought to try another bottle.'

'Shall I get off?'

'Not for a minute. If it was Gilbert, what do you suppose he was after?'

'I think it was a map. I'd borrowed it.'

'Rig, I'm sorry but he's about to explode. I can read the signs. Looks exactly like you.'

'Thanks.'

'When you were his age. That should have inoculated me against fatherhood. He's even got the same colouring.'

'Nobody else in the family has.'

'You're throwbacks, the pair of you.'

'Hi, George, join the club. It's very select.'

'Don't be long, Rig. We'll finish this later.'

'Yes.' But, 'Wait, Ben.' His eyes had been on Gilbert's map. His decision was spontaneous, and it surprised him. 'I think I'll stay here.'

'Once this scion of my loins is asleep, he's out for nine hours.'

'George isn't the reason. It's this stuff of Grandfather's. I'll keep in touch.'

'Can we upgrade that to a definite promise?'

Rigby hesitated, but the request did not come from a parent wanting to superintend him. Despite his seniority, Ben never pulled rank, and now he explained, 'I don't like to be entirely out of play.'

'I know. I'll ring you, if I get the chance.'

'Fair enough. All the best.'

Rigby replaced the handset. His stomach was as noisy

as George. He looked in the refrigerator, selected two rashers of bacon, a tomato and sausages, and slapped them into a frying pan. While they spat tetchily, he toasted two pikelets and ate the chocolate he had brought from home. Since preparation and consumption cost him a mere fourteen minutes, he was at a loss to explain how his mother contrived to take so long. Or how she created so much washing up. He sloshed water round the frying pan that had also served as a plate, found a used envelope and scribbled a promise to replace the food he had eaten, ending cheerily (such was the effect of the food): 'So, Grandad, watch this space.' But he asked himself, When? and for the first time he felt Gilbert's absence, the true emptiness of the house.

Now night was creeping round it, accompanied by wind. He could hear it in the trees, lifting their branches, tweaking away leaves, flicking them against the windows and carrying them into the porch to scratch on the flags. The beck was thrust along faster, rattling over its stones. Rigby switched off the light, opened the door noiselessly and listened. If Gilbert meant to return, surely he would come soon; it was rare that he ventured into the dark alone. He had once said, 'From my garage to the house is enough for me.'

On the beck path something skittered dry and brittle. 'Grandfather,' Rigby called, low, not wishing to startle. There was no answer. He walked quietly across the cut grass; when he came to the edge of it, something under a shoe cracked, a twig. 'It's only me, Rig,' he whispered, though he knew that Gilbert was not there.

For a time he remained, wondering what Gilbert was doing, whether he had booked in somewhere and would reappear tomorrow, unable to conceal his glee that he had caused this anxiety. 'You were a good lad to go to the trouble, Rigby,' he would say, and if Rigby were to point out that Carol had persuaded him and Ben had supported, Gilbert would not listen. He would make Rigby uncomfortable with excessive compliments, with flattery. As always, it would be as if his grandfather felt compelled to butter him up.

So, he asked himself, Why don't I lock up, hide the key under the water butt, and cycle to Ben's? Reason: Grandfather might not be at a farm enjoying bed and breakfast; he might be sleeping rough and I ought to start out early tomorrow to look for him.

Returning to the house he was astonished that in the darkness he misjudged the position of the porch and fell up the bottom step. Inside, he switched on the light again, relieved to see the familiar furniture and the walls that wrapped him against the night.

There were at least three hours left before he would usually consider dawdling towards his bed and this house offered no entertainment. Because of the hills, the reception on the radio was a jangling agony to listen to, and there was no television, no stereo, no computer, no bright paperback books. Rigby could not imagine how his grandfather got through the evenings. 'I've the gramophone,' he once pointed out, 'and you don't see many like it nowadays.' That was an understatement; you didn't see any. 'It's a valuable antique,' he had added, causing Rigby to plead silently: Please don't leave it to me.

The record that Gilbert and Carol had danced to that morning was still on the turntable. Rigby wound the handle and carefully placed the needle on the perimeter groove. After the first dissonant screech, someone announced, 'Take your partners for the fox trot,' and the band started up. It seemed suitable for the war-time dress that Carol had borrowed, whereas the uniform she had brought for him was so thick and rough it would have been stifling. Then he examined the map.

Backed by a fine cloth, it was more durable than the paper publications which soon split along the folds or, spread out, became as unmangeable as a kite in high winds. The scale was small, one inch to the mile, the more compact contour lines making the gradients appear unnaturally dramatic. The background was not white but a discreet pink and all the colouring was a shade darker. This made the map appear stronger, more positive.

It had been well used. In a margin Gilbert had scribbled 'Epsom' followed by numbers. Since the only information he had about Epsom was that it held a race-course Rigby assumed that the numbers were odds on a race. He knew little about racing and he had not suspected that his grandfather gambled. Nor had he imagined that, in spite of his claims, Gilbert had such an interest in the immediate neighbourhood. For, describing an arc six or seven miles from where Rigby sat, were five small pencilled circles. They conveyed nothing to him but since they indicated places important to Gilbert, they provided a basis for a search.

Encouraged, he fetched the ball point pen and writing pad that was kept in a drawer in the kitchen and began to work out a route. One place ringed was further west than the others and he decided to find it first. There, in the font used for 'Antiquities, non Roman,' was printed 'Abbey, site of.' But it was several miles from the one he knew, a grand ruin above the dale's river where grass and sandy beaches attracted picnickers and tourists. Sceptical of Gilbert's skill in map reading, Rigby wondered whether he had really intended to mark this abbey, but he discarded the idea. It was unlikely that Gilbert would make such a mistake.

He was considering the position of the next circle when the dance band slowed up, the fox trot limping in plaintive rallentando. He strode to the gramophone, lifted the needle and watched the record groan to a halt.

Its sound was replaced by the telephone's ring. This time there was no need for caution since everyone at home believed he was with Ben. So he answered, 'Hello. Rigby Cade here.'

No one replied.

'Who is that?' he demanded.

The silence continued. He felt it crawl along the wire. It filled the room, seeped through the stone of the walls, overpowered the wind and stilled the beck. The window was blank, a square of unrelieved black. He put down the handset, rejoicing in the sharp click, then he drew the curtains and switched on the electric fire. Its warmth was fringed with chill.

He returned to the map but he was unable to settle. He could not concentrate on planning the next day. The circles on the map were meaningless. Exasperated with himself, he jumped up and grabbed the telephone, dialed impatiently, jerked his head to a thought rhythm as he waited for Ben's voice. It told him that he was about to ring.

'Someone did about ten minutes ago.'

'Probably a nuisance call. Some person could have been checking whether there was anyone in the house.'

He had begun, 'Could it have been Grandfather?' but Ben was continuing, 'According to the local rag, the only print I can manage to read when I'm giving George a bottle, there's an epidemic of burglary where you are.'

'Thanks, Ben. I really appreciate that news.'

'*The Messenger*'s definition of epidemic is an incidence of two. Vandalism is on the up and up as well.'

'Anything else?'

'Let's think. What could there be? We've had foot and mouth disease and floods, so that leaves a dash of bubonic plague and a bomb on the Americans at Menwith Hill.'

'Shouldn't you be a bit worried about leaving your little bro out here all by himself?'

'I am. I doubt whether I shall get through tomorrow without counselling.'

'You haven't considered leaping into your car and racing over?' He frowned, admitting that the question was not entirely light-hearted.

'I'm not a free man. I have other cares. You've heard him.'

'I can't now.' Rigby was grateful for the shift of attention. 'Down for the night, is he?'

'Definitely. He's OK as long as he has a good yell before retiring to his cot. Where will you sleep?'

'I hadn't thought.'

'I don't imagine Gilbert will mind if you borrow his bed. We all have to make sacrifices. But it's not too late to cycle here.'

For a moment Rigby considered. He had done what he intended, verified that his grandfather had not returned. He said, 'You mean, now you've got me windy?'

'Have I?'

'No more than before. This house is a bit spooky. All this stuff of Grandfather's from years back. There's a cap badge and a lance corporal's stripe and centimes and letters addressed to Grandmother.'

'He was in the D-Day landings.'

'I thought so. And his map's odd. I don't get some of the things he's written on it.'

'Want to bring it along?'

'No, thanks, Ben.'

The room was quiet again as soon as he put down the handset and, turning off the electric fire, Rigby cupped the switch in his palm to muffle the click; drawing the curtains, he lifted their weight to reduce the scrape of the rings along the rail; locking the door, he turned the key slowly, and jumped at the inevitable snap. 'I'm securing the house,' he said aloud, but fear of burglars was not the reason he was holding his breath. It was Gilbert's possessions on the table. They made him nervous. And he had shut himself in with them.

The alternative was to walk along the beck path, in the dark, then cycle to Ben's, wake him up, say, 'I've chickened out.' That was impossible.

In his grandfather's bedroom he opened the window, let in a gusty draught. With it came a few tawny leaves and a brown gliding moth. The sheets on the bed were a tangled mound; he unknotted it and, without wincing, he shook up the pillow that still bore the imprint of his grandfather's head. It carried none of the disquiet of those possessions downstairs, souvenirs of a hidden past. When he had placed the map over them, it had not lain flat but was raised by their concealed shapes. It reared at the folds, mimicking the rise and fall of the land drawn on it, land eroded into valleys by ice and water, cracked and lifted by subterranean forces. Or – not valleys but troughs, trenches. Scored into the ground. And – not green heights grazed on by sheep but sour unnourishing earth, broken, tossed by explosions.

It was some time before he slept.

Four

He woke before light with the immediate recollection of where he was and what he was to undertake that day. Resisting this, he closed his eyes, even produced a reverberate snore. Its effect was to start him running through his repertoire, from melodic fluting and sibilant whistling, through throaty creaking to the full-blown deafening cacophony of labial pops, snorts, and startled explosions. It went down very well with George who would stop screaming, stunned with wonder, and attempt an imitation. Ben pleaded, 'Just restrict the show to *snoring*, please. That's all I ask.'

The memory made him lonely, the bed lumpy and uninviting. The demands of the new day grew assertive. Rigby got up, dressed, went round the house drawing curtains and made himself a breakfast sandwich – a fried egg slapped between two grilled pikelets. The latter seemed to be the central feature of his grandfather's diet. He spread margarine on four others, added cheese and pickled onion and built a respectable savoury burger. The milk that remained in a small plastic container was judged palatable, a robust mature dairy beverage, according to the after-sniff. This and the pikelet construction would provide quite a tasty lunch, though dainty. He distributed the items in the pockets of his anorak and moved to the table to collect the map.

Underneath it was the rest of his grandfather's private property. Sorry that his mother was not there to witness him, Rigby began to tidy it up. He had replaced the coins and other small oddments in a bag, had retied the ribbon round the letters and was attempting to push the documents into the card wallet when he felt an obstacle. He pulled it out. It was a sheaf of written pages, feint-lined and thin. The first was headed, **Fighting in Normandy, June 1944**. The handwriting was his grandfather's.

Rigby read: **A message to Dr Fenella Dixon**, and he thought: Why should Grandfather write to a doctor? He would boast, 'Sound of mind and limb, that's what I am, with an iron constitution.' About to replace the pages in the wallet, Rigby caught sight of the words: transit camp, roads jam-packed, convoys, me and a gunner. Intrigued, he read the first lines.

I've decided to have a shot at describing what happened. As far as I am concerned, it's over and done with, but you have said you would like to read about it so I thought I had better see what I could do.

There is a matter I want to straighten out first, Doctor, and I hope that you will take it right, no offence intended. When you have read what I have to say, my wish is to have it back. It is a question of confidentiality and so far I've had no reason to doubt that's not observed, but once something goes on paper, there is the impression created that it is being handed over. Well, that is not so. What is written here belongs to me and I would rather keep it that way. It came at a cost, I'm not talking money.

Here goes, then.

Rigby told himself, 'I shouldn't be reading this. It was meant for Dr Dixon and no-one else.' But his eyes had not stopped. They were already on the next paragraph.

There had been rumours swilling round the barracks that something big was in the pipe line but nobody knew exactly what or where. Training tightened up. People talked about the Allies invading France since that seemed the only way to put an end to the war, if we came out on top, that is. It was when we were despatched to a transit camp, first leg of the journey, and then to the marshalling area, beginning of June, that we got the measure of what we were in for. That was because of the weight of movement. The roads were jam-packed with convoys of lorries and equipment and you would see trains carrying nothing but tanks and guns. Security was stepped up. In the holding camp near our embarkation point we were not allowed to send letters or use the phone; we were briefed on our bit in the campaign and French money was handed out. There was an excitement, of sorts, this being what we were trained for, but the old hands had more the attitude, the sooner started, the sooner finished.

Me and a gunner put back a few pints the night before we went on board the destroyer detailed to ferry us across. It was his twentieth birthday. I said to him. 'Here's to you being back in civvy street before your next birthday.' He said, 'I've made sure of that,' and showed me the talisman he had stuck on his watch strap. I do not recall his name but I remember his look, more begging than hopeful, and I wondered if my feelings showed so clear. I was not many months younger than him.

Next day we boarded the destroyer but the sea was rough, there being something of a gale, so we were held up. D-Day was put to June 6th, a day later than planned, and the gale calmed down a bit. Not enough for the troops, though. We weren't natural seamen and it was not long before we got the brunt of the swell, a few miles off the Normandy coast when we had to leave the destroyer. We filled the landing craft that had been hanging from davits and we were let down over the side and into the sea. The waves were so high you thought that any moment they would swamp you, take you to the bottom. There were thousands of craft all making for the same stretch of beach, some were going under, struck by enemy fire, and there were mines and wire and iron contraptions we called hedgehogs armed with explosives and lined up on the sand. Only those were not the first things you saw when the landing craft emptied you into the sea, four feet of it in my case which had the advantage of rinsing off the vomit. The water looked like it does if you throw a grenade into a river, the fish float up stunned, only it was not fish kept banging against your legs, it was men. They were the first killed I saw in Normandy, and they were ours. The waves were nuzzling round them, then gathering them up, laying them on the sand and stroking over them back and forth with the incoming tide, back and forth.

I came in a bit after the first assault troops which is probably why I'm here today. You could see what the first lads had been faced with by the state of the beach, Sherman swimming tanks were brewed up, landing craft turned turtle and washing in, armoured vehicles knocked out, bodies and wounded everywhere. A mortar was firing down the beach. You put your head down as if that way you'd make less of a target, and ran, not as fast as you'd like, having boots filled with sea water and your trousers clinging to your legs like sodden sacks. There was no end to the stuff coming at us. When a chap thumped down there would be a call for a stretcher but I doubt if it was heard, the noise being what it was. The order was, No stopping, and I obeyed it. At least, that's what I said to myself on the day, but the truth was I wasn't made for heroics and I wanted to stay alive. It was later I would have willingly made the swop.

Behind the beach were dunes and a flail tank going like a windmill, its chains were throwing up the sand and exploding mines. We took the path it made. Back of the dunes was a little village. At least, that's what they said it was. 'Had been' was more exact. It had taken a pasting early morning, before the invasion started, and I don't know the state of the rest of the seaboard area, but this village was practically blotted out. It was the first example we met of what they called RAF and navy support, and it was a shock. There was hardly a wall left standing. We didn't see any French. I expect they had evacuated the place as soon as they got the first shell, but there was still room for snipers.

There's nothing makes you so nervous as snipers, though I must say we all shook a bit when our Typhoons ripped in, nearly took your head off. Like the Yanks, our boys were not above making mistakes. Rockets and machine guns scare the pants off you and a German Mark 4 tank with its 75mm gun pushing out of a hedge can have you screaming inside and scratching your way down to Australia, but a sniper is nasty, hidden, and you could be the chap in his sights. That morning one took out three of us before we located him, behind a bit of trellis against the only wall left of a school. They went down together when we threw grenades. 'Well bowled,' Lieutenant Crosby congratulated. 'It was Stanley's that got him, mine went wide,' I told him. I didn't want to get a name for precision lobbing though as it happened it was the one thing I could swank about. In the army it's advisable to take a back seat, anywhere else can lead to trouble, like being volunteered for the daft risky jobs.

I'm happy to report that it was not long before we grew somewhat astute about snipers, when we were in open country, that is. And the reason was, they would post themselves up trees. When we realised that, a lot of trees were sprayed with rounds that had never harboured as much as a pigeon let alone a German. Then Rufe pointed out that we could distinguish the trees by the scratches on the bark made by the boots of the sniper as he climbed up. 'There's no need to tear into a decent tree,' he said. It was him, too, that discovered snipers would often strap themselves to a branch so they had both hands free for the rifle. Once, he had to be ordered not to cut the man down. The sergeant's language would have made the devil blush. 'That's a Gerry sniper hanging up there, not a Red Beret.' He'd had a cousin with the Airborne in Sicily.

I've been a bit previous writing about snipers up trees, so I'll get back to the first day. The enemy had been taken by surprise, not expecting landings in Normandy, but though the RAF bombs and navy shells had knocked out dwellings, they had not finished off all the batteries, nor blockhouses. The little seaside towns were so many fortresses, the houses strengthened with concrete and turned into gun positions. We had to clear out remaining defenders. But I doubt if we did, entirely. The Germans had systems of trenches linked up and underground passages to retire to when ground level got too hot and I have to say that there were many occasions when we envied them.

What you need to understand is, the first day was a shambles. (I don't know why I specify one day, I don't recall many that weren't, but on the first day they were struggling to get some organisation going.) As we stalked through the streets behind the sea front, we kept our eyes skinned for enemy defences, all the time climbing over rubble and trampling over rolls of barbed wire. That was in addition to what had got its ticket after escaping being shot up on the beach. Vehicles and men. Often it was only by the colour of a shred of fabric that we knew whether they were ours or German. I recognised one by the talisman he had glued on his watch strap. The sight churned up my innards worse than the sea crossing. 'Leave it,' Lieutenant Crosby said but he scraped up a handful of dust and scattered it over. 'Pioneer Corps will see to him.'

Those early days, there was never any let up. When the seaboard area was in our hands we felt a bit safer, our men at our backs, but as we advanced inland, the enemy was forever mounting counter attacks. (I speak of our company, understand. Some of our troops had reached target on schedule, soon there were chaps in Bayeux, and the Canadians, God bless them, were outside Caen.) But wherever you were, I can say without contradiction that you were filthy, uniforms rough with salt once the sea had dried off, and hungry, your box of rations soon finished and Catering Corps not yet under way, and you were living on cigarettes. I owed Rufe a packet by first night. Normandy started the habit. But worst of all that was the absence of sleep. We had forgotten what it was, kept awake by bennies that were handed out. Bennies was our name for pills of benzedrine, which is amphetamine. We weren't the men that had boarded the boats in England. We were zombified, as my young grandson would say . . .

Rigby paused in his reading. He had not before seen himself mentioned in any writing except once at first school when, asked to list primary colours, Liz Bonniwell had put, 'Rigby's hair.' Then, instead of his usual outrage, he had felt secretly pleased to be picked out by a little girl who could recite the thirteen times table, execute a mean tackle in football, and gave generously of her packed lunch. This morning the reference to him was disconcerting.

Perhaps that is why I kept near to the bloke already mentioned in connection with the snipers, the one we called Rufe. He was an uncommon sort of chap and thick set, on the heavy side, though he lost the excess in a matter of weeks. He was better at soldiering than I was. You learn on the hoof and most in the first month, provided you don't get your ticket first. Some of us picked up the tricks of the trade faster, and one was this Rufe. He did not get so zombified as some of us did, and I'll give you an example, but before that I have to mention the noise.

It never let up. Even if things had gone a shade quieter where you were, in the neighbouring sector there would be a racket. When we were miles from the coast we could still hear the shelling coming from the navy. There was the thunder of bombers trying to knock out German positions, and the rattle of the armoured brigades and as you went in to attack there were the explosions of the fire carpet our gunners laid in front of us, and the animals bellowing in the fields, and the pigs, and the horses screaming, near death, trapped in their harness. (The Germans transported some armour on carts.) So you'll appreciate there was never any real quiet in Normandy. Never the quiet of a place resting, breathing soft. If you ever got the sense of it, as if all of a sudden you were back at home, early morning, awake before the milkman had delivered, with everything still and silent, you had to pull yourself up, remind yourself that kind of peace was suspicious. As like as not, it was a sham. It cost one of B section his life. I was with him, along with three others.

The light on the page was altering; it was more diffuse. The morning had begun. Rigby switched off the lamp. Reluctantly he replaced the sheets in the wallet, then he pulled them out, found a plastic carrier under the sink, wrapped it round them and crammed the little parcel beside the milk and sandwiches. Still thinking about what he had read, he stepped out of the house.

And saw that the waterproof cape and spade had been removed from the porch.

Five

Disbelieving, he stared at the empty hook and the gap by the stacked logs. He recalled Ben's joke, 'There's an epidemic of burglary,' then, '*The Messenger*'s definition of epidemic is an incidence of two.' But this person had not broken in; he had been satisfied with an old ripped cycle cape and a spade when what they would fetch at a car-boot sale was not worth the trouble of carrying them away. A more likely explanation came to him: his grandfather had returned, wishing to spend the night in his house, the thought of its welcome cheering him as he fumbled along the path. But, finding the door locked, all the warmth he could claim was a cape, and the only assistance for tired steps, a dirty spade. Rigby said to himself: If my guess is correct, he has had to sleep rough, as he did in Normandy; but now he's an old man. He winced at the idea and, walking to the water butt at the side of the house, he left the key in its usual place.

He walked down to the beck. The previous day he had ignored the plank over it, wedged there many years before. 'Ready for when you want to play on the other side,' Gilbert had said then, to forgive Rigby's avoiding it, 'I can see our little bridge has got a wobble. I'll attend to it.' But discouraged, he never did. This morning, as Rigby stepped on the narrow timber, he was sorry that his grandfather could not see him.

He had to collect his cycle, for 'Abbey, site of' was several miles away, but instead of taking the path by the gill, he decided to make a detour along the top of Beacon Height. It bulked opposite the house, its base shadowed by the trees. The morning's misty breath slicked their bark, the shed leaves of many autumns formed layers of damp mush. Rigby grasped saplings to haul himself upwards until the trees ended and he was in bracken. Above him was a harebell blue sky. Striped with clouds too sparse to shutter the sun, it released him from the dank wood, from the untenanted house, from the shock of Gilbert's narrative, from the concern about his unsheltered night. Invigorated, Rigby rushed at the ascent, felt the flex of the muscles in his calves, the pump of his lungs, the channel of sweat down his neck as he watched the peak of the ridge draw closer. Until, with a grappling spurt, knees ground upon boulders, fingers clawed at gritty roots, he was at the top and lay panting on grass and the pale bran of its seeds.

Eventually he stood up. Over his shoulder, the moor was a brown, rusty expanse, too wide to show him the lane that led back to the house where he lived. In front of him was the country of Gilbert's map. All the places he had ringed on it lay here. Rigby examined it. The beck and the house were hidden by the wood but he could see the road beyond them. Light pricked between trees when the sun caught the windscreens of cars. Their movement created a busyness but their noise did not reach him and their passengers were unseen. Bordering the road, the meadows were empty. There was no solitary figure.

Scanning further, Rigby made out The Grand Old Duke of York and a straggle of hikers crossing the bridge over the river. His eyes followed its course. It lay mild and thin as a summer stream, distance concealing the speed of its flow and the sections of foaming turbulence. Long before it disappeared under the spread of fells, all details of terrain and creatures were beyond the stretch of his vision.

Although he did not truly expect to catch sight of Gilbert, he kept glancing below him as he strode the length of the ridge and scrambled down its steep spur. So, preoccupied with his grandfather, it was he that

Rigby first thought of when, entering the lane, he heard his name called.

'I saw you,' Watkins announced. 'So I thought I'd better wait. You going this way?'

'That's right.'

'In a hurry?'

'Right again.'

'I don't mind.' He adjusted his steps to Rigby's stride. Accusing, he said, 'Last night you were supposed to be going to your brother's. What's his name?'

'Ben.'

'You said you couldn't pace me with your bike, not even a couple of miles.'

Rigby did not answer.

'I don't believe you had a bike. It was just an excuse.'

'My bike's where I said it was.'

'So how come you're here? What's this lane got that's so fantastically interesting?'

'You ask a lot of questions, Watkins.'

'I bet you never went to your brother's. It was all a story to get out of lending me a hand.'

'It was legs you needed a loan of.'

'You might have had the courtesy to tell me the truth. I can take it.' He looked at his watch. 'It's only zero eight fifteen hours. Seems a bit early to be walking on Beacon Height.'

'I'm an early riser. Now that *is* a lie, Watkins.'

'Have you got something special on, then?'

'You could put it that way.'

'So have I, though I would have appreciated an extra hour's kip, after that drag last night. Have you ever had to walk down this lane when it was pitch black?'

'I can't remember.'

'In other words, you haven't. Well, I can tell you it's not nice. Not nice at all. You're vulnerable, that's what you are.'

'What to? Wild animals?'

'Motorists. And bikers. As soon as it's dark, they rev up and take to the road. In their thousands. Convoys of them.'

Rigby laughed.

'You wouldn't have laughed. The minute they've got you in their sights, they hoot. If you don't jump into the hedge, they run you down.'

'I don't notice any damage.'

'I twisted a foot. Makes the going harder today. You couldn't slow up?'

'No.'

'All this kit is a handicap. It weighs 16.4 kilos. That's average weight for the infantry, *and* I've got this tent. I'm on a twenty-four hour exercise.'

'Is that another bright idea of your dad's?'

'He's the expert. Everything has to be absolutely kosher, no matter what the cost. See this rucksack? Genuine issue. And the boots; I'm not grumbling they're a size too big. Then there's this combat gear. What do you think of it?'

'I'm not sure it suits you.'

'The camouflage is very subtle. I'll show you.' Accoutrements clanging, Watkins ran ahead and crouched in the grass.

'I don't think it's quite subtle enough,' Rigby told him.

'Perhaps it works better if you're further away.'

'I'd be happy to have a go.'

They had reached Bonniwell's farm and Rigby opened the gate.

'Don't try that on again,' the other shrieked. 'Pretending you've got a bicycle.'

Before he could answer, someone shouted, 'I'll bring it,' and a bell tinkled.

Rigby smiled at Watkins.

A girl came round the shed; she was trundling two cycles. 'Something on this is crying out for oil,' she announced and sent Rigby's speeding towards him. He caught it before it crashed. Noticing Watkins, she greeted, 'You may come forth, Henry. I can see you.'

He explained, 'Rigby's going to check what the

gear's like further away. You're looking very . . .' he cast round for a compliment and hit upon, 'ready for business, Liz.'

She glanced down at the crumpled track suit and flicked dried mud off a cuff. Keeping her expression sober, she mused, 'I'll probably rinse this through before Heather Dale's party. Is that what you're practising for?'

'I wouldn't go in this,' he told her, horrified. 'I couldn't take the risk.'

'You don't have to worry about people seeing you. Heather's lighting, she hopes, will be very subdued.'

'Have you been invited?'

'My mum's helping.' It was a sufficient reason. 'Look, I've got to get on. We're playing Holly Garth this morning and the bus is picking me up in less than ten minutes by New Bridge.'

'We'll pace you, Liz,' Watkins offered and began a gentle running on the spot. 'Is it a netball match?'

'Yes. Area semi-finals.' Addressing Rigby, she asked, her tone urgent, 'Going that way?'

As they mounted their bicycles, she answered Watkins, 'I'll take you up on the pacing bit another day, when I'm not so rushed. And when you've dumped that clobber. I didn't know you were in the Army Cadets.'

'I'm not. I'm . . .'

Already moving, she called back, 'Do you carry an entrenching tool?'

'What do you know about them?'

'Not much.'

When Watkins, vigorously waving, was behind them, Rigby asked, 'What's an entrenching tool?'

'What it sounds like. Soldiers dig trenches with them, and a whole lot more. So Mr Fenton said.'

'Who's he?'

'He stayed bed and breakfast last night. What I wanted to ask you, Rigby, is whether your grandad is ill or anything. They deliver his *Messenger* to the farm every Friday and he hasn't been to fetch it.'

'He's gone missing.'

'No! I wondered why you'd left your bike.'

He described the situation.

'I'm so sorry. Mr Miller is sweet. Whenever he passes the farm and I'm in the barn practising the sax – Mum won't have me doing it in the house – he stops to listen. He says I ought to take it up professionally.'

'He knows nothing about playing the saxophone.'

'So what?'

'He'll say anything to please.'

'At least he's showing an interest. Where are you going to look for him?'

'I've got a number of leads.'

'There's been an old man at the bottom of the lane but he wasn't Mr Miller. This man who stayed bed and breakfast last night, Mr Fenton, came across him.'

'When?'

'After one o'clock this morning. He got lost coming down from Penrith. Now he's gone, making for London. Some people have all the luck.'

'This person could have been Grandfather.'

'I don't think so. He jumped up and shouted as soon as Mr Fenton pulled into the side, thinking the old man had had an accident, only he went on at Mr Fenton, calling him a road hog. Mr Fenton would have driven off but the man was leaning over the bonnet, waving a spade. That doesn't sound like your grandfather.'

'I think it was.'

'He's not like that, bawling at the top of his voice and being violent. In any case, I wouldn't have thought he knew one end of a spade from the other.'

'During the night, Grandfather took one from his porch.'

'I don't believe it!'

'He's the most likely suspect.'

'I mean, Mr Fenton thought he was going to swing it at the windscreen. He felt really threatened. He began to reverse, only there's mud, and the drain, so his wheels went into a spin; they wouldn't grip and the car was waltzing about. Then the old man dashed to the back, making a terrible din, and Mr Fenton thought he was being attacked in the rear.' She laughed suddenly. 'That's what he said, "I thought I was being attacked in the rear," and Dad said, with not a smile, "There's no danger from the Scots nowadays, not since the Lady Anne built her tower." Anyway, the noise was this old man trying to get his spade under the wheel. By the time they had the car clear, they were friends. Now that does sound more like Mr Miller.'

They had reached the main road, were standing behind The Grand Old Duke of York where Liz had propped her cycle against a wall and was fixing a padlock and chain. 'At the end of it, this man advised Mr Fenton to keep an entrenching tool in his boot, it being a piece of equipment with more uses than digging yourself a foxhole. Or out of it. But he wouldn't accept a lift from Mr Fenton and afterwards Mr Fenton wondered whether he should have telephoned a hospital or something because, before he drove off, this man said to him, "I'll give you another tip. There's a river ahead, and if the bridge has been blown up, get hold of a Churchill AVRE and it will drop one over. Takes thirty seconds and works like a dream. I've seen it done." Was Mr Miller ever in the army?'

'Yes. Second World War.'

'That's centuries ago.'

'I think he was only just old enough. They were called up at eighteen.'

'Our Trev will be eighteen before he leaves school.'

'I hadn't looked at it that way.'

'I wish I hadn't. Rig, I reckon you're right to try and find Mr Miller, get in before, before anyone can . . . I mean, he doesn't do any harm, does he, living by the beck. There's nothing wrong with him, is there?' She was pleading, wanting his denial. 'Knickers, the bus is coming. Look, if there's anything you want me to do, let me know. Take my phone number.'

'I haven't got a pencil.'

'Right.' She unpinned her team netball badge and scratched the numerals on a bench outside the public house. 'Learn that,' she ordered as the bus drew up.

Owned by the school, the bus ferried parties to concert halls, theatres, camps, stadia, sites of dubious interest and, on Saturdays, it delivered to games fields. Today it carried a banner extolling the unbeatable prowess of the travelling team who confirmed their fearsome qualities with hoots at Rigby and noses squashed, pug-like, against windows. To demonstrate the futility of this sexual harassment, he raised his eyebrows, stretched up and tapped a glazed nostril. For a reason unrevealed to him, this action triggered cheers and waves.

He thumbed, Good luck. Drawn into the ethos of school, he was lighthearted, but as the bus disappeared over New Bridge he thought of his grandfather's advice to Mr Fenton, imagined the piers collapsed into the river and the peelings of tarmac, limp, serrated, sagging down the banks. He told himself: Grandfather did not truly think it could be blown up; he was joking. But he was not completely convinced.

He memorised the scored telephone number and got on to his bicycle. Cars went by him and a man driving a lumbering tractor signalled him to pass. He had taken on this job and he would get it over as soon as possible. Then he could go home, lounge about, watch the football match, call out Tim for a game of squash, endure his family. Freelance living was fine but it was long on responsibility and short on company. Even so, when he saw a figure, rucksack and tent bobbing, he gave it only cursory acknowledgement and stood on the pedals of his cycle, urging it to go extra fast.

Six

For most of its length, the road that led to the Abbey, site of, was no more than a lane running between hedges and across the muddy entrances of cowhouses. Where it was bordered by a rough moor, it was unfenced, crossed by cattle grids. However, the position of the abbey was clear, beyond the apex of a sharp bend, but reaching this, Rigby could see no signpost or stile, only a path that led to a house.

'Have you lost yourself?' a voice addressed him. It came from somewhere between a pair of Wellington boots and hands that pegged out washing.

'I'm looking for an old abbey.'

A head pushed round a sheet already plumped with wind. 'Don't tell me you're another.'

'I could be.' Another. He got off his cycle and laid it on the grass.

'There's not a soul interested, years and years on end,' the woman smacked the sheet aside and squelched across the grass, 'then we have two in as many days.'

'When did the other person come?'

She repeated the question, trying to filter out its significance. Giving up, she told him, 'Yesterday. Round tea time.'

'Thank you.' He was at least sixteen hours behind Gilbert.

'You know him, then?'

'If he's who I think he is.'

She laughed. 'Aren't you the cagey one? Why's that, I wonder? He's a real gentleman. "What a beautiful garden," he said to me. Of course, he was referring to the border.' She pointed to a few browning chrysanthemums and some balding roses. 'I keep on top of that. The rest goes to pot nearing winter.'

Rigby nodded agreement.

That was a mistake. Cross, she told him, 'There's a lot of work. It's not like something you can get through, evenings, after a nine to five job, and mine's round the clock. The other one didn't need that pointing out. He'd seen a bit more of the world than you have. "I'd regard it as an honour," he said, that's exactly what he said, "I'd be honoured if you would make me a gift of a single rose." ' Repeating the request cured her sharp tone. ' "With your permission I am about to visit where the abbey stood," he said, "and a rose out of your garden would be prettier than any plastic poppy." '

'I see.'

'Do you, now? I don't. Well, not altogether. Have they started sticking poppies in the back of beyond? Not that we mind, but they should ask permission.'

'I don't think it's official.'

'Roses or poppies, they won't last long, what with the sheep.' She spoke as if the creatures were liable to stampede, iron pattens buckled to their hooves.

'Is it alright if I have a look?' he asked her.

'So long as you don't start a fashion. The abbey was somewhere behind the house. The old gentleman knew his way; he'd been here before, he said, but I've never seen him. There's nothing there, except for the monks' well. Hasn't been for centuries. I expect the stone was taken for building, and why not? Better to be put to use.'

Though Rigby had not expected picturesque ruins, he had hoped for a stump of a pillar, a gargoyle grinning out of a bed of nettles. There was nothing to indicate a building had once stood there. The monks' well, too, was disappointing; it was a pond banked by bushes, saved from stagnation by a trickle of water that drained through. Rigby could not imagine what possible interest the place held for Gilbert.

The pond was roofed by trees. Under them, and among the bushes, the grass was high. Where he stood, many of its stalks were bent over; they had not yet recovered from the crush of a person's tread. He followed this pale track.

And discovered, threaded through ivy that wound over an ash, a flower. What petals remained were limp and at a more advanced stage of decay than those left on the bush in front of the house, and impaled on the stem was a piece of paper. It was a plain page torn from the end of a diary and headed: *Notes for June 1944*. Diagonally across it in his grandfather's hand were the words: You found her beads in the rubble and took them to the wounded nun.

Rigby leant against the bole of the ash. The strange pain in his head told him that he was holding his breath and he let it out slowly. Then delicately, without causing another petal to fall, he rearranged the rose so that it did not droop. He could not guess who was the 'you' in Gilbert's dedication but as he returned from the site of the abbey he thought of its chiselled stones that had fallen and been pillaged for building and of the villages shelled to rubble along the Normandy coast.

He was picking up his cycle when the woman came out of the house and called, 'Seen the well, have you?'

'Yes, thanks.'

'Have you any more thoughts on whether you know the old gentleman?'

'I know who it was who came.'

'Will you be seeing him?'

'I hope so.'

'In that case, you can give him something he left. I'll fetch it.'

Rigby walked up the path and waited. He could hear children playing. One ran to the door and, holding the bell of a tricycle, rang it viciously, his head cocked waiting for Rigby's reaction. He obliged, squinting his eyes, lolling out his tongue. Less appreciative than George, the boy ran shouting for his mother. There were reprimands, the sound of a television, and all other noises ceased.

'I invited the gentleman in for a cup of tea. He was looking under the weather,' the woman told Rigby, handing him a cigarette lighter. 'I don't know why he had that; he didn't smoke, just sat over his tea with it in his hand.'

'I'll see that he gets it.'

On his cycle he rode slowly although knowing he should not delay. He had been right to deduce that the circles on the map might lead him to Gilbert but when he stopped to choose the next, instead of the map, he drew his grandfather's account from his pocket. Straddling his cycle, he unwrapped the little package, looked through what he had read and continued.

We had been detailed to search a farmhouse. It was as big as a regular hall, high and grand, standing one side of a great yard like a quadrangle and the other sides mostly filled in with tall barns, stables and such. We went into them first, observing the proper procedure, nothing there except a few chickens scratching. Then we tackled the house. The door was unlocked and had not a dent in the wood, the whole place had escaped the bombardments. It was a miracle.

We tiptoed in making no noise. We were in the kitchen with a great fireplace and pans hanging, a long table and not a speck of dust. In the middle of it was a jug of milk. None of us leaned forward to pick it up, take a swig. Through the window we could see clothes, soft and clean, pegged on a line. We stood, resting. There was not a scrap of sound. It seemed that if we stayed long enough, the war would go away. Then Peter said, 'I'd forgotten what quiet was. Better check upstairs,' and he walked through the door. But that did not quite break the spell. What did was a shot, and Peter slithering down. Immediately a German stood in the doorway, a revolver hanging in his hand. His jacket and collar were unbuttoned, he had been enjoying a nap. He said, and his accent rang clear as a crystal glass, 'I suppose I should take you prisoner, Troopers, but what in the world should I do with you? The only solution is—' and as he raised his gun to his head, a round from Rufe went through his throat.

We carried him and Peter to a barn and laid them side by side. Then Rufe shouted, 'Doesn't it bother you I've killed a prisoner?'

When little Ted pointed out that the German considered we were *his* prisoners, Rufe said, impatient, 'That was bravado. He would have been ours eventually.' By that he meant, after we had overcome him, and no doubt one or more of us getting the cop.

I reminded him that the German intended to shoot himself anyway, and Ted told him, 'Gil's right. That's what the man wanted.'

'But not *how* he wanted it,' Rufe snapped.

'Look,' the sergeant came in, 'we're not running a Jesuit seminary, we're fighting a war.' (I do not give all his words, Doctor, you being a lady.)

The truth was, we were all rattled. We had not known who that officer was aiming for when he raised his gun and he had time to kill at least one of us. He'd seen Peter out. Germans and Allies knew that death was measured in the slimmest shaving of a moment. If you took breath before squeezing the trigger, you didn't take any more. It did not matter that in that sliver of time we saw that the officer was aiming at himself. Three of us had taken that breath. No wonder we didn't feel inclined to give Rufe a hearing. Quibbling over the finer technicalities was less important than the fact that our fingers had not moved.

Sergeant Theaker said, 'My report will state a German officer was holed up in the farmhouse. We entered without incident but he resisted being taken prisoner. Understood, Rufe?'

He flushed up. 'There's no need to ask.'

'Just making sure. I'll keep the Walther.' It was already in his pocket, he having the highest rank. Unfortunately, he did not keep it long. It went to Ted soon after and I was the last to have it. Sergeant added, 'That is, if you have no objection,' as if sorry to be spoilt of one.

Ted bent down and straightened Pete's jacket. 'Look at it this way, you ugly sinner,' he told him, he had a job spitting out the words. 'You're lucky to be stretched out in one piece, and tidy in a barn, nice and comfy on a bed of straw.'

'He'll get a proper burial,' Rufe comforted. 'The French are respectful of the dead.'

Rigby looked up. Coming towards him was a figure. It wore combat dress but carried no rifle. Carefully Rigby parcelled up the pages. As he replaced them in his pocket, his mobile phone bulged, demanding. He brought it out, saw that a text message waited: Nuz plez. C.

Then Watkins came to a halt beside him, greeting with: 'We must stop meeting like this.'

'Spare me, Watkins.' Steam blossomed in the valley below them and carriages rattled. He asked, 'Have you come by train?'

The other was piqued, which was satisfying. 'You don't seem to realise I'm on an exercise. You might even call it survival practice. Anyway, that train was leaving too late.'

'So you did consider it? Cut out a chunk of walking?'

'Part of survival is to have initiative and command your environment. So I called at the station for a timetable, but I can tell you I'm glad train travel isn't allowed.' He spoke without conviction. 'I mean, the journey's only five miles and the rate that engine goes, it would be quicker to walk, as well as the carriages being full of people who get a buzz on smoke and whistles and steam. Frankly, I think it's an overrated experience.'

'You're lucky to miss it, then.'

'In any case, I'd have been taken out of my way.'

Rigby smiled. 'That's another compensation for obeying orders.'

The other snapped, 'And what are your orders, Rigby?'

'I don't have any.'

'You're filling in time, are you, till she comes back from the match?'

'Who?'

'Liz Bonniwell. Why didn't you go along to cheer?'

'You're talking stupid.'

'She obviously fancies you. That's where you were last night, visiting her place. No, don't give me some story,' he anticipated Rigby's interruption, 'it won't wash. Else your bike wouldn't have been at Bonniwell's this morning, would it?'

Rigby was silent. This argument was suggesting possibilities. He reflected on them.

'I mean, when you think about it . . .'

'That's exactly what I am doing.'

'. . . it's obvious.'

Rigby grasped the handlebars of his cycle, prepared to move off, but Watkins did not shift. He asked, 'Would you be good enough to let me use your mobile, Rigby? I ought to be giving my Dad a call now. He's spent hours working out the route, timing each section.' He was looking at his watch. 'He is monitoring all stages.'

Rigby handed him the phone.

'I'll just text him. That'll cost you less.'

'It also avoids questions you might not want to answer.'

The other responded, stiff, 'Speak for yourself,' and Rigby murmured silently: You've got a point.

As he returned the phone, Watkins saw the cigarette lighter still tucked in Rigby's palm. 'I didn't know you smoked, Rig.'

'There's a lot of things you don't know, Wat.'

'It's a bad habit to form.' He ran through the risks with relish, ending, 'My father wouldn't let a cigarette into the house.'

'Do you have many trying to force their way in?'

'You can smile, but you could face a horrible future. Bronchial complications alone can put you out of effective action, you can get so you have to have an oxygen mask.' His breath caught and he began to cough.

'You really should cut down,' Rigby advised.

'It's all that smoke at the station.'

'It must be. You've no antibodies against it if you've got a Pure Air Dependence.'

'I might have a cold coming. I didn't feel too good

when I got up, but I said to myself it was probably nerves.'

'Watkins, I'm sorry, but I don't want to stand here gossiping about your psychological condition. The subject's too big and I have to get on.'

'You're surprised by me referring to nerves, but I've never done anything like this before – spend twenty-four hours covering the miles, except for the ones in the tent – and I don't want to disappoint Dad.'

'If I were you, I would chance that. He's not your sergeant major.' He looked at the combat dress, the gadgets hanging from the belt, the rucksack, the roll of tent, the boots that Watkins had said were too big. 'Now, if you wouldn't mind stepping to one side.'

'What's all this riding about in aid of?'

'You've explained I'm filling in time till Liz returns from her match.'

'You haven't admitted it. I've told you what project I'm on.'

'I hadn't noticed we'd signed a contract.'

Watkins attempted an unconcerned shrug and fixed his eyes on the cigarette lighter. 'May I have a look?' he asked. 'It's an old fashioned one.'

Rigby held it out.

'What I thought,' Watkins announced. 'I bet you don't know the troops gave this name to Sherman tanks.'

'You're right, I didn't.'

'You see, this lighter is a Ronson.'

'Is it?'

'Yes. And Sherman tanks brewed up faster. My dad told me. They were used in the Second World War.'

'Was he in it?'

'Do you mind? That would make him old enough to be my grandad! But he's made a study of it.'

'I'll bet.'

'And I bet you're dying to know why the troops called Sherman tanks, Ronsons.'

'And you're dying to tell me.'

'The advertisement for Ronson lighters was: They light first time. A shell or a mortar hit a Sherman, and . . .'

'I've got the picture.'

They were silent. Rigby was thinking: Grandfather saw that. He asked, 'How many men did they hold?'

'Five. If you were lucky, if the hatch was still working, you might get out, but not generally everyone, before . . .'

The early mist had gone; it was a bright autumn morning. The sun was on Rigby's face, and his eyes through glowing lids saw his fingers locked on a metal handle, the blisters rising and the skin darkening, peeling away. Flames punctured his jeans, consumed the hairs, skewered his private parts, while his rib cage swelled with smoke, with the fumes of oil and cordite, of cindered flesh, and his mouth was a black hole, open, out of which no more screams came.

Watkins said, 'Enough to send you batty.' He stepped back, adjusted the straps on his shoulders. 'I'm afraid I can't stay any longer. I have to do a loop – up Great Fell then descend to this road further along. They aren't shooting today?'

'If they are, you'll soon know.'

'Dad's checked, but I wanted to be right up to date. You aren't by any chance going in that direction?'

'I could be.'

'That's a slice of luck. You could do me a favour.'

'I'm contemplating a change of plan.'

Watkins persisted. 'Do you know where the path from the fell enters this road?'

'No.'

'It's by a gill – How Gill. You could take my equipment to there.'

'Well thanks, but I'll have to decline the treat.'

'I don't see why. You don't have to trudge up that fell.' He stabbed a finger towards the distant slopes.

Then with one sweep of an arm he levelled the lane's steep gradient. 'When you're cycling along here, it would be no burden.'

Rigby put a foot on a pedal, was ready to go.

'It's not much to ask. It's not as if I'm asking you to go out of your way.' The other sulked, accusing.

'Look, Watkins, I have to consider your father's plans; I just wouldn't be able to square my conscience.'

'I reckon Dad would be tolerant. One has to be a bit of an opportunist, and I've got a blister coming on this heel.'

Rigby did not believe him but he said, 'Shut up, and I'll take it.'

He had to suffer the gratitude, the toadying compliments on his generosity, the instructions: 'Would you please leave it two or so metres off the road, and cover it with bracken.' To which he answered, feeling a fool with it strapped to his shoulder, 'Sure you wouldn't prefer me to stand guard?' Then he had to push off, the pack rigid on his back, the tent scraping his neck, leaving Watkins unencumbered, jaunty as a green recruit marching to a bloodless war. Unaware of the true reason why Rigby had agreed.

He had not been persuaded by argument but by the recollection of Watkins' white face as he had said, 'Enough to send you batty.' And because his fingers had shaken as he turned the cigarette lighter over and over in his palm.

Seven

By the time he reached the cattle grid, Rigby was so hot he would have sworn that he was accompanied by a nimbus of steam and followed by a trail of sweat. He could understand Watkins's eagerness to pass on his clobber and he considered dumping it on the grass and pedalling away, but he paced out the requested two metres, flattened some bracken, dropped the pack and tent and covered them up. As he finished, three motor cyclists ripped past. One slowed down, with a studied bravura swung round, and returned to Rigby.

'Burying someone, Rigby?' he asked.

'That's right. A sheep got its wool ravelled up in my front wheel.'

'Must have been on its last legs.'

'That's exactly what I told it. Afterwards.'

The young man laughed.

'You're not about to say, "Race you to the main

road," are you, Goff?' Because he remained sitting, straddling the bike.

'OK, isn't it? Just done a ton up this lane.'

'Lucky there weren't any more sheep crossing.'

'Like a ride?'

'Not unless you can tow my cycle as well. But, thanks. Some other time.'

'I'll be going then,' Goff mouthed through ear-shattering revs. Then, removing his foot, said grandly to encourage Rigby, denied such a charismatic conveyance. 'Won't be so many years, Rig, before you can join the fraternity.'

Goff's leathered back receding down the lane was impervious to Rigby's scowls.

He sat on the mound he had made of Watkins' rucksack and examined the map. First, tracing where he had travelled that morning, he found that the new stretch of road that he and the school bus had taken was not marked, yet the old one was, now disused, and near it was an incomprehensible addition: a hospital. This was shown as an antiquity, printed in the Gothic font. More strangely, the railway line was not limited to the five-mile stretch preserved by railway enthusiasts whose steam trains Watkins had deplored. Instead, it continued, curved, ran south, took a way whose evidence was still visible – an arch over a lane, a level swath of gritty earth under a bridge, an unaccountable embankment across a meadow — until it joined the present line at the town where Rigby lived. Above the station, on the moor slopes, a golf course was marked but, closing his eyes, peering into the bracken, scrutinising the ridge and the path to the ancient, incised stone, Rigby could see no remains of tees or bunkers. The moor had reclaimed them. Then he looked for the road to his house; it did not exist.

It was as if he had turned a corner, was faced with a gap that offered not a trace of walls, doors, his bedroom. Not even a heap of masonry. He felt disorientated and for a moment he panicked, lost touch with the day, with himself. Then he went to the bottom of the sheet, read: 'Mounted and folded, 3/-,' and the date, 1947. No wonder the map did not record places as he knew them; it bore the evidence of people, their travelling, their homes, their landscape that belonged to another age. But he had to follow it.

After a time, he looked for the lane he was on and related it to the other circles Gilbert had drawn. One was quite close but its position was less clear than Abbey, site of, for the scale was too small to pinpoint the exact location. The area probably measured several acres.

Rigby cycled to the end of the lane, crossed a wide road, went through a gate, parked his bicycle by the hedge and looked round. He was in meadowland through which ran the river; he had not seen this since leaving Liz. Across it, on the slopes, was a plantation of firs. It would provide thorough concealment. But the place ringed was on Rigby's side of the river and here the only trees were a few oaks standing majestically alone, commanding their space. The rest of the meadowland's expanse was empty except for the occasional interruption of a wall and, not far distant, a barn. Rigby could see that its roof was sound. Partially hidden by a rise of the land and far from the paths used by hikers, it was sequestered, a dry shelter.

Rigby hesitated because for the first time he realised the full meaning of the task he had undertaken: to search for a man who had chosen flight. The alarm of his family now could be described as interference. Had he not himself often wanted to go off? Then he remembered Liz's account passed on from Mr Fenton of an old man on the road, his spade translated into an entrenching tool; and he thought of Gilbert's account of the Normandy invasion, a part of his life he could confide only to a doctor, a stranger. Whatever Gilbert's state of mind, Rigby was not confident that he could deal with it and he swore at Carol and Ben for leaving him to cope. The resentment covered his fear. Approaching the barn, he decided that, if

Gilbert repulsed him, he would not argue but just turn about.

The doors were slightly open. He called, low, almost in a whisper, 'Grandfather?' When there was no answer he pushed on the latch, widened the prying shaft of light. On the sill of the small, high window a jackdaw protested, then flapped away. No one lay on the thick plastic sacks; the remnants of stored hay were too wispy and sparse to make a bed; there was no footprint in the floor's dust. Instead of disappointment, Rigby felt relief.

It did not last long. For sensing something behind the half opened door, he peered, tilting his head out of the strong strip of light. Wedged in a cairn of stones were two pieces of lath. They had fallen from the roof and were lumpy with the droppings of roosting birds. On each one, neatly tied with twine, was a twig newly snapped from its branch. He was looking at two crudely fashioned crosses.

Rigby sat down, his heart pumping, and stared at Gilbert's memorial to two men, one having shot the other and himself shot by the soldier called Rufe. Hiding the cairn in this unfrequented place, Gilbert had hoped it would not be disturbed and he had taken a handful of hay and brushed away his prints. To test the ease of it, Rigby gathered up a few stalks and erased his own.

The crosses made the barn solemn. Though Rigby was hungry he could not sit and champ through his lunch. It would have been like eating in a church. Nor did he feel that he could simply walk away. So, selecting a plastic sack, he sat down, took out his grandfather's narrative and found his place.

We had set up a camp of sorts in a hamlet. The residents had fled, along with thousands of others. (Where they all went I haven't the foggiest notion but they undertook the journey despite the likelihood of being pinched between our troops and the enemy's. Once things were quieter they tramped back with the livestock they had rescued, their carts weighed down with kiddies and blankets and pans.) You could sympathise with them for being on the surly side with regard to what the fighting had done to their homes and fields. Not to mention the cattle and other animals. You did not have to be a countryman to near weep when you saw cows racing round after catching a shell, mad with pain, butting their heads at trees, anything left standing, and bellowing. Screaming. We would try putting the poor devils out of their misery till we found we had swopped noise for the stench of the carcasses. As I've said, we could sympathise with any Norman that was hostile, considering what had been done to their land, but most were very welcoming, especially once we were properly on the move. They would line the streets and cheer and the girls would grab chaps and hug them and kiss them, notwithstanding the muck and the sweat. They would bring jugs of milk, and bread straight out of the oven that tasted sweeter than any I've had before or since.

I got sidetracked again, Doctor. What I was planning to describe was one night sometime after we had left Peter in the barn. It was hot and I could not sleep, despite the longing for it. I got up, had a word with the men on duty and went for a stroll. It was not dark; we were nearing the summer solstice which made it possible for both sides to start fighting early and finish late. I've never known such short nights as those we had there.

There was the usual noise of squadrons going over, shells and explosions. Taking the track that led out of the village I was soon under trees. Their leaves curtained off the flashes in the sky, the darts of tracer, and they changed the long daylight into dusk. For the first time since D-Day I was by myself and, what is more, I was on a track I could not see the end of, in a country I did not know, and if our patrols had skimped their business, there could be, assembled ready to attack, a battalion of German infantry armed with

Schmeissers and field mortars, along with the full division of Panzer Lehr. In fact, I was on the point of making a quick retreat, my mind was so taken up with these nasty fancies, when I caught sight of downright evidence of them, and I froze. Couldn't move. A figure was crouched by a bush and hovering on top of it was a tin hat. Then I saw it had not the shape of a German helmet.

'Ah, it's you, Gilbert,' a voice said, and I recognised it as belonging to Rufe.

'You scared the living daylights out of me,' I told him. 'It was like I was seeing a headless ghost.'

'There are plenty about, but I'm not one, yet.' He had stuck his tin hat on the stock of his rifle and was holding it above the bush. We would do that from time to time in order to entice a sniper, and if he fell for the trick and fired a round, we had him located.

'I haven't drawn any fire so far,' he remarked.

'Have you heard any movement?'

'No.'

'Then why have you pushed that up?'

'I saw you coming, Gilbert.'

I told him I didn't understand what he meant and he said I was to forget it and, 'Don't let me detain you.'

If I had been the age I am now, I would have walked off, but at nineteen I could ignore a snub. I said,

'I wasn't going anywhere special,' and I sat beside him on the grass.

I tried a few openings for conversation. He didn't take any up till I mentioned Peter. I remarked, 'We were all a bundle of nerves.'

'That wasn't through nerves,' Rufe corrected. 'It was negligence.'

'He forgot the drill.'

'He was careless. Peter would have agreed.'

I asked, 'You knew him pretty well, then?'

'No better than anyone else.'

'Anyway, you settled the account.'

'Don't assume I shot the man to avenge Peter. I did it for myself.'

'And me and Ted and Sergeant Theaker have you to thank for it.'

'Then you're wasting your breath.'

It could be hard going to try to have a talk with Rufe. 'Defending yourself is an automatic reaction,' I said, ignoring the fact that the reactions of the rest of us had missed a beat.

He did not answer.

I remembered what he had said immediately after the shot, so I asked him whether, given the choice, he would have let the officer shoot himself.

'You ask a lot of questions, Gilbert, but never the

right ones. Such as: Did I shoot the German because I wanted to, wanted to kill? Or did I shoot because I didn't want to be killed?'

It was my turn to be silent. The questions were for him to answer. They had not occurred to me, and I did not like the thought that one day I might be facing them. We had been given a job and we wanted to get it over with as fast as we could. It sickened me to consider there might come a time when I enjoyed ramming in the bayonet. I said to Rufe, 'I hope it never gets so either of us answers "yes" to the first question.'

'I hope so, too,' he agreed, and for a few minutes our thoughts were shared.

'You asked whether I would have let the German shoot himself if I'd had the chance,' Rufe said. 'I reckon I would have done. You should take a man seriously that wants a bullet in his head. If that's the way he wants to go, then he should be allowed.'

I had not listened to this sort of talk before and I was not comfortable with it. It screwed up my guts. The man it came from was no more than a month older than me.

'You seem to have given the matter some thought,' I remarked, wanting to put an end to the subject.

At this point, the bottom of the page was frayed; a strip had been torn off. On the next page, the sense did not follow on. It was: 'It'll not come to that,' I said. I had never felt so mournful.

Perhaps the sheets are not in the correct order, Rigby thought, or one is missing; but he did not search for it. The questions of the soldier Rufe disturbed him and he did not wish to reflect on the man's disinclination for Gilbert's company. 'Don't let me detain you.' . . . I could ignore a snub.

So, quickly, he pushed the sheets into the bag, telling himself that he had stayed in the barn long enough. Miserable, he trudged over the meadow, collected his cycle and was in no mood to tolerate Goff and his cronies when he saw them on the Lady Anne's bridge.

Eight

The bridge was narrow, therefore when a car approached the three bikers had to give way. They speeded down the slope, waited until the car had passed then went through the usual routines. Goff demonstrated his skill at kneeing which Rigby reluctantly acknowledged was quite respectable, but he scorned the tentative wheelies and stoppies of the other two.

They had returned to the top of the bridge when Rigby reached its base.

'You need some puff for that, Rigby,' Goff shouted.

On any other day he might have answered, 'You're right,' and have started to pant, laboured against the incline, slowed down, tottered, guyed alarm at the imminent fall, let his cycle slant, then recover precariously. Or he might have slid back, tried to conquer the bridge with a brave spurt of speed, and when he finally attained the crest he might have wiped his forehead, asked one for his helmet, and passed it round. But today he pressed hard on the pedals, glided to the top, pulled up a smidgen short of a gleaming mudguard and stated, 'Sorry, nearly scratched your zimmer frame.'

The owner yanked the wheel away and cautioned, 'You want to watch out.'

Goff said, 'You have to make allowances, Col. He's envious.'

'Not of that.' Rigby contrived a cauterising scorn. 'It's rubbish. A jumped-up moped.'

'What do you know about it?' Col demanded, now on the defensive.

'That model got the thumbs-down at the last Birmingham show.'

'Nothing like what your model's going to get,' said the third and grasped the bicycle's handlebars with a thick gauntleted fist.

'I hope your trike's insured,' Goff commented. Then, 'Hang on. The SAS just dropped in.'

Watkins was approaching them. The respite from carrying weight had refreshed him and he was striding rhythmically, achieving a good pace. A khaki beret that he had added to his outfit was worn at the regulation angle and the roll of tent lying at his shoulders increased his width.

Stewart jerked the handlebars, asked, 'Friend of yours?' because Watkins had waved to Rigby and as usual hailed him.

He said, 'Take your filthy mitten off my bike.'

At this point exchanges grew muddled. Watkins, not acknowledging the others, asked Rigby, 'Coming my way?' Stewart said, 'Not on his bike he isn't.' Watkins added, 'Thanks for taking the pack,' and Goff asked, 'Was that what you were burying, then, Rigby? Should have cremated it,' and Watkins commented, 'There's no need to be offensive,' and Col explained, 'That's our Goff being polite,' and Goff asked the uninterested sky who Watkins thought he was.

Col said, 'He's in the Boy Scouts,' leaned from his motor cycle and flicked a thumb at the tent, asking, 'Is this a marquee or a teepee?' while Goff corrected, 'Not Scouts, Col, army.' Watkins declared that he was a member of neither and Stewart explained to Goff that the army did not take recruits until they were eighteen which prompted Watkins to clarify with: 'You can enrol at the Army Foundation College when you're sixteen if you wish to become a combat soldier.' This caused Stewart to unlatch his grip on Rigby's handlebars, paddle his bike to Watkins and after a thorough scrutiny of his features pronounce that he was lying: he was never sixteen. Watkins then pointed out that he had not claimed to be attending the college; he had merely given the lowest age they accepted students.

Then Rigby shouted, 'Leave it, Watkins. Let's get going,' and to the others who were now corralling Watkins with their bikes, 'Move it, will you?'

There was no response. Stewart's attention was fixed on Watkins' being a student, Goff's on his being in the army, and Col on his belonging to the Boy Scouts . . . not that he had anything against them, as such, but he could suggest better ways of spending time than poncing over the countryside in fancy dress.

'You're a cadet doing a little traipse, aren't you, Sunshine?' Goff intervened and argued that the army was strong on giving aggro, it was one of its brain-washing techniques. When Watkins attempted to sort out misunderstandings, his voice tight and pompous, Stewart interrupted with: 'Listen to him. No squaddie talks that way. He's a student. What you here for, Brainbox? Giving the grey matter a rest?'

At which Rigby raised his voice and thundered, 'Break it up!'

Their noise stopped; their heads turned. Stewart said, 'And what if we don't?'

Rigby's fingers gripped the pads on his handlebars, the nails biting in. 'That's obvious.'

The three glanced at each other.

'Rigby!' Watkins wailed.

'You keep out of it.'

Goff said, 'Do as Sarge says, Soldier boy.'

Rigby ordered, 'Just move your bikes so he can get past.'

'It's restricted steering on this model,' Col told him, 'being as it's rubbish,' and he turned his wheel three degrees.

Rigby stared at the invisible gap, felt his breath quicken, his nostrils flare. Words exploded: 'You great thickie, believing you're so big because you've got a bike, do anything, no one to stand in your way. Except you still have to be in a gang.' His wave included the others. 'Ratio of three to one. It's pathetic. You'd soon pull out if the odds were even. You measure guts by numbers. And anybody can see why: you haven't a working muscle between you. More than a two-mile trek would give you heart failure. You wouldn't have the bottle to try sleeping rough. And this one's asked what happens if you don't shift. I can show you. See this boot? In one second flat it can shatter a faring.'

Immediately the three paddled their bikes out of range.

'That was uncalled for,' Goff rebuked. 'We were only having a bit of fun.'

Stewart ran through his repertoire of oaths, none of

them original, and finished with: 'He wants a lesson taught him.'

No longer hemmed in, Watkins moved to Rigby's side.

Col assured Stewart, 'No probs,' and swung off his saddle.

Goff said, 'You can count me out.'

'You, what?'

'Some other time, may be. When he's got less tongue. I don't fancy tangling with a maniac. Anything could happen.' He patted the gleaming paintwork of his bike. 'He's got a reputation for temper.'

That was rapidly ebbing away. 'You first,' Rigby said to Watkins and low, as he followed him, 'Just take it easy. Don't run.'

'If I tried, I'd be brought down by this pack. Will they come?'

'Two might. Not Goff.'

'How do you know?'

'He wouldn't want to risk spoiling his chances with my sister.'

Aghast, Watkins said, 'She isn't interested in *him*?'

'I couldn't say. Women have funny tastes.'

'But he's got bleached hair!'

'Carol might go for his motor bike; they often do. The important thing is, he thinks he's in the running.'

'It's a good thing you were there. Things might have turned out nasty.'

'They were doing before you arrived.'

A van met them, halted at the bottom of the bridge. The three on its crest were obliged to start up their engines and speed down the other side.

'Here, off the road,' Rigby ordered, lifting his cycle over a wall.

'That's not my route.'

'Please yourself. I don't fancy a couple of motor bikes snapping at my back wheel.'

'You shouldn't climb walls,' Watkins reprimanded. 'It's against the country code.'

'Use the gate further along then, but you'll have to sprint.'

Hesitantly Watkins laid his hands on the top stones, complaining, 'I'm not properly balanced for this.' But he succeeded cleanly and fast when Rigby put a hand under the rucksack and supported its weight.

Below the wall, the field shelved down to a small gill. Trees hid it from the road. 'I don't suppose they will see us here.' Watkins was asking for reassurance.

'If they did, they wouldn't trust their bikes to it. The place is a scrap yard for boulders.' He had to carry his cycle through them, slipping on the silted leaves. 'I'll give them a quarter of an hour.'

'They're crazy.'

'I riled them.'

'They deserved it,' Watkins declared, slithering behind him. 'Getting at me like that.'

'Before you arrived.' He had provoked them, so they had turned on Watkins. 'I've already told you.'

Deaf to Rigby's meaning, the other persisted. 'I appreciate your support. You really laid into them. I wish I had such a command of vituperation.'

'Blimey! I didn't know I'd got that.'

'It's the first word that springs to one's lips,' Watkins claimed, smug. 'I'm pleased it wasn't directed at me.'

'There's still time.'

'You put your finger on it, them not knowing what it's like to do a good tramp, because you go in for that yourself.' Tactfully Watkins removed his eyes from Rigby's bicycle. 'I agree that they wouldn't consider sleeping out. So ignorant! "Is this a marquee or a teepee?" one asked.'

Rigby smiled. It occurred to him that he might find Watkins less irritating if he had a touch of humour.

'Of course, they don't know anything about the army.' He pronounced the last word with a capital A. 'Jeer at it. They are nothing but a set of lily-livered wimps, the sort of spineless cowards that let other men go out and do their fighting for them.' Noticing that

Rigby was sitting, he relinquished invective, which Rigby suspected was his father's, plomped down and concluded weakly, 'They get up my nose.'

Rigby was tempted to say: Feel free; they aren't listening, but the other might interpret this as an invitation and he did not wish to hear any more on the subject. He was ashamed of himself for not controlling his own outburst.

So he asked, 'Do you plan to join the army?'

'It's a good career, and the country has to have one. Else what do we do if there's a war?'

'I'm not sure I'd want to train for something that might never happen.'

'That's the point.' Leaving Rigby no time to question the logic of this assertion, he continued, 'There are peace-keeping assignments, too.'

'That seems a contradiction to me.' He saw the other's expression and added, 'Joking, Watkins.'

Watkins nodded, tolerant. 'You get to see the world.'

Rigby thought: Particularly the parts that war is bashing up . . . this village was practically blotted out . . . There was hardly a wall left standing . . . climbing over rubble and tramping round rolls of barbed wire . . .'

Watkins was saying, '. . . no end to the skills they'll teach you. Like mechanics and orienteering, and driving tanks and such. The equipment is very sophisticated. They move with the times. It's a tremendously efficient organisation. Have you ever considered joining the army, Rig?'

'Me? Are you trying to be funny?'

'It's not a subject to joke about.'

I recognised a gunner by the talisman he had glued on his watch strap. The sight churned up my innards worse than the sea crossing.

Interpreting Rigby's silence, offended, Watkins said, 'You tell me what else I can do, living where we live.'

'If you're after an outdoor life, there's drystone walling. You could chisel yourself a little niche in that.'

'I'm sorry you can't be more serious.'

'Look, you've plenty of time yet. It's ages before GCSE.'

'You should have a target.'

'Provided it's the right one.'

'Mine's that alright,' Watkins declared, but he turned his head, examined a grey feather swirled in the miniature rapids of the gill. Finally he demanded, 'Otherwise I wouldn't be on this project, would I? It's a sort of test, see. It's been very carefully organised.'

'Did you have any say in it?'

'Of course I did. Dad paid a lot of attention to my

contributions.' But he did not name them or suggest that any had been adopted.

Rigby said, 'Goff and company should be out of the way by now.' He picked up his cycle and, as a concession to the other, led him to the gate.

'The coast's clear,' Watkins reported. 'No sign of the enemy. I have to go up river now before moving south and setting up camp. Quite a trek.'

'It would be more comfy to stop off at the bunkhouse,' Rigby encouraged rebellion.

'The arrangement has been made. Where are you making for?'

'I was thinking of doing a ton along the top road.'

'You don't need to waste any more time,' Watkins told him, sarcastic. 'She's come.' A landrover had passed them and pulled into the grass verge. Watkins ran to the passenger door and, before it opened, called, 'How did you get on?'

'We won.' Liz Bonniwell jumped down.

'Congratulations.'

'Thanks. We played a cracking game.'

'I can't speak for the rest of the team, but I know you would,' he answered gallantly. 'Unfortunately I have to move on; I've a schedule, and I'm running a little late.'

'Dad will give you a lift if you'd like.'

'I appreciate the offer but I'm going along the river path.'

She nodded. 'It's very soggy. What you need is a bobbin tank. That would lay a lovely strip of canvas in front of you.'

'I've never heard of them.' Seeing her smile, he protested, 'You're having me on.'

'No. You should run a B&B, Henry. It's amazing the things you pick up. Anyway, if you don't mind, I have to have a word with Rigby.'

'Rig? Oh, yes.' He affected surprise at Rigby's appearance. 'I'll leave you, then.' He adjusted his beret, stuck his thumbs under the straps of his rucksack and strode away.

Looking after him, Liz told Rigby, 'I reckon I know what his problem is.'

'Which one?'

'He wants to be liked.'

'He has a funny way of showing it.'

'I don't think so. Do you suppose he knows how much people talk about him? I would hate that.'

Rigby thought: Watkins would say, Liz, your name is forever on our lips. Instead, he asked, 'Did the match finish late?'

'No. Dad had to collect some feed from Marsden's, so he called at Holly Garth and took most of the team for lunch at The Prize Heifer. He claimed the landlord would be proof against the shock.' She tapped on the driver's window, said, 'Please don't wait for me, Dad,' and the landrover drew away.

'Have you had any luck, Rigby?'

'I've found traces, but not Grandfather.'

'Dad's told me something I thought I ought to pass on.'

Nine

Liz explained: 'Dad had a call early morning. Our Dalesbred had found a gate open and were all over Miry Moss. Dad got Victoria and Albert into the landrover and went to round them up. Some of them had scrambled through the fence into High Wood before they realised it didn't offer their sort of nosh, then they couldn't get out. Dad had a dreadful job because Vicky's still only a pup and was no use at all. In fact, she got a couple of ewes into that old derelict building not far from Pickles Gill.'

'Which derelict building?'

'Dad says it was put up during the last war; he doesn't know why, but the story was that the people who worked in it were engaged on something very hush-hush. People let them be, not wanting to get involved. Though I suppose the barbed wire fence helped.' She laughed at the idea and Rigby joined her. After the last twenty-four hours, to laugh seemed like a new experience. 'Anyway, Dad had to go into this place to fetch the ewes out and he saw a cycling cape. He says that it didn't look as if it had been there long.' Moving into a deeper register and adopting a more pronounced regional accent, she quoted, "More *fresh* is how I'd put it, not having the look of a garment that had seen the inside of a cow parlour." ' Resuming her own voice, she said, '*Fresh!* A cycling cape!' and laughed again, then said, not irrelevantly, 'I've just played a really good game. Mr Miller has a cape; I've seen him wearing it. So I wondered whether the one Dad saw might belong to him.'

'His has gone.'

'Since when?'

'Some time last night, when he took the spade.'

Liz was now thoroughly serious. 'The building is quite a way from his house.'

'Not as far as other places he's been to. I don't know how he's managing to get to them.'

She nodded, not asking him to explain, concentrating on this find. 'He might have gone to this one for shelter. We did have rain during the night.'

'Yes.'

'But it's not at all dry. The roof leaks and all the windows are out. It's horrible. And it stinks.'

'I'll have to go, have a look. How do I get there?'

As she directed him, describing a short cut, Rigby realised that she was helping him to find the area enclosed by another circle on Gilbert's map. 'I think he knows High Wood,' he told her. 'Though of course that doesn't prove it's his cape.'

'There's a good chance. I'll keep my fingers crossed.' She turned, was reminded that the landrover had gone and exclaimed, 'Knickers! I'd forgotten. Still, gives me a chance to walk off the lunch.'

'It's miles.' Probably six, he calculated, and would have suggested she came with him and shared the bicycle, but he had to search in this neglected building alone. He said, 'You take the bike.'

'I can't do that. I'm not looking for Mr Miller. You need it.'

'I shan't be able to use it to reach this squat – whatever it is. So I'll be dumping it very soon, then I'd have to go back to collect. A bike can be a hindrance. Won't you take it, Liz?'

'Since I'll be doing you a favour,' she accepted, amused. 'I might even investigate this click that it's got.'

'I haven't noticed.'

Wondering how he could have been so abstracted, he watched until she had crossed the bridge, then he turned and continued up the lane. It rose sharply, affording a view of a long stretch of the river. Far away, on the path beside it, was a figure, bulky, moving fast. It occurred to Rigby that whenever he looked for his grandfather, it was Henry Watkins he saw.

The route Liz had given him was in the opposite direction and soon he had left the lane and was tramping through plashes where water faltered, or where, spreading thinly, it converted the ground to a sponge. On such terrain it was impossible to maintain a good pace. He told himself that he would do better if he were not starving and that he ought to eat the savoury burger, but he did not stop.

It was some time before Rigby reached High Wood. Climbing the fence he was apprehensive, unable to imagine why Gilbert had abandoned the 'fresh' cape. Under the trees the ground dropped shallowly to a thin gill. It flowed indolently, hampered by fallen leaves. He jumped over it, tripped and found that his toe had been caught in a noose of wire. It was attached to a concrete post that had collapsed, was covered by grass, and from it more wire looped upwards to other posts still standing. Their tops angled towards him, high, festooned with steel barbs. Behind these, he could see a construction that was probably a water tank and, further back, the building he sought.

One storey, it was built of bricks that were streaked with verdigris slime. The step to its only door was broken; plantains grew in the cracks. Walking along its length, peering through window frames jagged with splinters of glass, Rigby looked into a line of cell-like partitions divided by plywood that was bowed by damp. Beyond these was a corridor, then more toothed window frames in the further wall. At last entering, the door off its hinges, he knew only by a few links of chain hanging from a cistern where the lavatory had been; only by pipes and a number of split shelves, where a kitchen had stood. He turned into the corridor, trod through fallen plaster and puddles scummed with its dust, aware of a smell that touched his memory but could not be traced. At the doorway of the last stall he stopped, stood for a moment before he entered, walked to a corner and, as if reconciling himself to a theft, he picked up the cape.

It was dewed with moisture. A seam was ripped. The smudge of white paint at the hem had been made during some childhood mischief. Rigby could see himself grabbing the brush from the tin, racing away with it, gleeful, dabbing at the cape hanging on its hook, and Gilbert running after him, his mouth wide with laughter. He had not been wary, looking askance at his grandson, waiting for him to judge his pleasure.

The cape was not truly for cycling. It was a rectangle, big enough to protect a pack; when the opening was unbuttoned to the hem, it could be laid flat and used as a ground sheet. Rigby shook off the drops and, at full stretch, folded it, guided by the lines that had formed as it had hung from the peg. Then he saw that the cape had not been forgotten but deliberately arranged, for the place where it had been was not wet or dusty but covered with brittle leaves, twigs, a handful of blonde grass. He bent down and poked, found a small cylinder of paper, feint lined and flimsy, the inky strokes of his grandfather's handwriting showing through. Rigby unrolled it, held it like a scroll to prevent its curl springing back. One edge was frayed; the piece had been torn from the page.

About to read what it held, Rigby paused. To stand there longer was uncongenial; the walls were greasy with damp and the floor was gritted with sediment from plaster and brick. Also, he wanted to escape from the stench. No doubt the cause would be lying behind the building. He knew what it was and, led by his memory, he walked towards Ingleborough, came to the passage of Trow Gill where it was, lying on its side, its eye sockets empty, its fleece sodden and heaving as a thick skein of maggots worked. He would have tried to cover it with earth but there was none, only stones and nettles, and the stench, trapped in the narrow trough, forced him to nip his nostrils together and race away.

Now, Rigby strode down the corridor and over the crumbling step.

Although he was eager to examine the scrap of paper, his stomach forced him to eat first. Strolling under the trees, he took out the savoury burger. One mouthful told him that cold pikelets are nauseating. He lobbed a chunk at a pigeon; it declined the treat and flapped away. More hungry than the bird, Rigby chewed, trying to manoeuvre the cheese and pickle in his mouth to be the dominant tastes, and mainly succeeded. The milk would not have passed Mr Bonniwell's criterion of freshness, but its shortcomings were less pronounced if it were tipped fast down the throat. After this, he chose a shrub behind which to relieve himsef, grinning that he should observe the convention when there was no one to see him.

With the root of a beech as a saddle, he leant his back against the trunk, took out his grandfather's narrative, turned to the page with the slice removed. Then, taking the slip of paper he had found under the cape, he placed the torn edges together. But however much he fiddled, they would not fit. Frustrated, he dismissed the puzzle and re-read the last lines: 'You asked whether I would have let the German shoot himself if I'd had the chance,' Rufe said. 'I reckon I would have done. You should take a man seriously that wants a bullet in his head. If that's the way he wants to go, then he should be allowed.'

I had not listened to this sort of talk before and I was not comfortable with it. It screwed up my guts. The man it came from was no more than a month older than me.

'You seem to have given the matter some thought,' I remarked, wanting to put an end to the subject.

Then the page ended with the tear. The next began:

I said, 'It'll not come to that.' I had never felt so mournful.

That was not only because of this conversation with Rufe, Doctor, but because the last weeks had been an eye-opener. You see, in training, before you've been in a proper engagement, you never put two and two together, meaning it's always the enemy you think will go down, never you yourself – the skin you stand up in, the sparks along the nerves, the brain clamped in your head can never come to harm. But once you're in the thick of it, you learn otherwise, fast, and it's a shock. The enemy isn't one of your mates pretending to be on the opposite side, he's got a gun with real rounds in it and he's out to drop *you*. And you get so as when other chaps stop the bullets you ask, why. Why them and not me? I still ask that question.

I expect you'll have heard the saying, Doctor, 'All's

fair in love and war.' Well, it's a lie, on both counts.

Getting back to events, I'll recount the first time our company had a taste of what the German Panthers could do. I remember it well, and what came after, the two things so different I could have been in another world.

Heavy fighting was going on to our south and our division was moving across country in support of armour advancing somewhere on our right flank. A patrol which had gone out that night had found no activity and we were telling ourselves this was a swanning job. In other words, a hitch on a tank, a few rounds from its 17 pounder and all we would be left to do would be bring in the prisoners. You will have guessed what I am about to say, Doctor, but we were exhausted through to the marrow. Or perhaps how we felt had something to do with the morning. For once there was not much noise and, being ours, it was friendly. Dawn was just lifting over the cornfields. It brought no smell of cordite or smoke, or dust. There was still dew on the grass.

It was soon mucked up. We were moving alongside fields, down lanes with hedges and trees that grew high and solid on top of earth banks. The name they give it in Normandy is bocage, and the tanks had a job getting through if they managed at all; the crews hated it. Rufe was perched on a Churchill ahead of me. When he dropped off, I did the same. Suddenly we did not seem to be swanning any more. The quiet was more like the sort that starts you thinking of graveyards. 'I don't like this,' someone said. 'I feel like Jerry's breathing down my neck.' He had barely got that out when he was thrown into the air simultaneously with a burst of fire and the tank he had been on exploded. The next three got the same. Those turning into the lane attempted to reverse, became fouled up and were sitting targets, while infantrymen tried to make themselves scarce. You do not take a rifle to quarrel with a 75mm gun. Not all of us succeeded. The Panther was 45 tons, which was enough to think about without its gun, and there was a line of them dug in behind the hedge so camouflaged they merged with it. After putting out our forward tanks, their guns swung round, sniffing out smaller prey.

I cannot say how many men we lost, or how many tanks went for a burton. Some of the crews baled out but not all could. To this day I'll wake in the night, hearing the screams.

After that, what was left of our company retired to re-form, as it's put, and a group of us got separated. Lieutenant Crosby had given the map reference but had neglected to hand over the map that went with it. 'We don't need one,' Rufe declared when an argument developed. 'He's shown us. That's enough.' Harry asked why, in that case, there wasn't a line of men slogging behind, and Ted remarked that he could not see any tracks of our tanks (left from when we advanced). 'We're going a more interesting way,' Rufe told them.

That occasioned some strong language. The upshot was, Harry announced that he was striking off and being a chap who liked a flutter, he bet a packet of Capstan that he would be holed up nice and snug before me and Rufe were. That was the opinion of the rest of them.

'Aren't you going with them?' Rufe asked me. He didn't take it as a compliment when I said, 'I reckon you're guaranteed the fags.'

Rufe led me along the sides of fields, mainly full of corn. It did not make for easy going and I had a boot giving me jip, but I did not mention it straight off. Neither of us referred to what had happened, the men we had lost. We would speak of them eventually, but not on the day. What we were remembering, then, was their last moments and for the time being we were bent on burying the sights. It is a necessary practice.

After a while my boot was grinding into my toes at every step. I asked Rufe if he could judge the future mileage. He answered that he could not say exactly but we were not lost. He had memorised the map.

I said that I could not look at a map and hold the features in my head enough to find my way about them and I considered that to be a remarkable feat. 'I reckon it'll stand you in good stead when you're back in civvy street,' I told him.

This was exactly the kind of silly remark that Watkins could have made, Rigby said to himself, and was not surprised to read Rufe's answer:

'You talk a lot of bilge,' he told me. Then he added, 'I'm sorry, Gilbert. I shouldn't have spoken like that.'

'Nothing to worry about,' I assured him. 'We're both on edge after this morning.'

He replied that he did not feel on edge at that moment. In other words, he did not accept my offer of an excuse for him being so insulting. Rufe was nothing if not honest. And I did not take the hint, explain to myself that the man did not much like me and would have preferred to get rid. Don't ask me why I did not. Cussedness, I suppose.

Anyway, for a time he was more friendly. 'Talking about civvy street,' he began, 'have you any plans?'

When I said I might stay in the army, he showed a genuine interest and asked, 'Doesn't this lot put you off?'

'A war doesn't come round every year.'

'It might happen more often than you've allowed for.' (He judged correctly, didn't he, Doctor?)

'Somebody has to do the job,' I pointed out.

'I don't see you as a professional soldier.'

As it happened, I did not see myself as one, either, and I like to believe that it was Rufe's influence that stopped me signing on, despite disappointing some elements in the family. 'I don't expect you will have considered it,' I remarked.

'Spare me, Gilbert. You talk as if the army is about the only career on offer. If it figured at all on my list, it would come at about two thousand and ten.'

(We were so very young. The grandson I've already mentioned can exaggerate like that.)

As when Gilbert had explained Rigby's fondness for 'zombified,' this reference to himself made him shiver.

I should have let the matter rest but in those days I had not learnt when to stop. So I answered, 'Whatever your opinion of the army, here and now you make a good soldier.'

'And you make a good bootlicker, Gilbert.'

'I spoke in all sincerity. You seem at home with it.'

'At home? With the army!'

I could not entirely explain what I meant. He gave the impression that he knew what he was doing, he had

115

confidence, it seemed he could anticipate the next move. (Remember, that morning Rufe was the first to drop off the tank; and he had been the one to shoot the German in the farmhouse.)

I told him, 'You've got an instinct.'

'Is that what you think I've got? That's rich. Very. Rich.' He laughed but then he stopped like a switch had been turned off.

We passed through an orchard, the apples were like little marbles and not ripe but we made a meal of them. Nearby was a dwelling. There had been some action round it, the ground was churned up and a shell had taken off a corner of a room downstairs; glass and pans and chunks of wood that had been furniture strewed the dried mud. A curtain hung in a tree.

'I hope the family got out before this came along,' I said.

Rufe made no comment. He was looking at a cow and a calf lying on their sides, legs stuck out, stiff, their stomachs swollen. We had to hold our breath against the smell. Rufe said, 'This wasn't recorded on Lieutenant Crosby's map.'

'It probably wasn't our armour did it,' I suggested, and he asked what difference it made whose armour it was.

We crossed a little stream. At the top of the bank

there were trees and the remains of a gun position. Rufe remarked that it commanded a good view of where we had just come from. In other words, if the gun hadn't been knocked out, we would have been picked off easy as ripe cherries. I could not grin with him. There were plenty of shell cases about but no bodies, so I insisted on taking my boot off to examine the blisters. Rufe rested his back against a chunk of concrete and closed his eyes.

Now, as well as looking at a map and seeing the ground as it was depicted, Rufe had another talent that was equally rare. He could snatch forty winks any place, any weather, for five or ten minutes and come out of it refreshed. That day I didn't consider he had chosen the most suitable moment. I cautioned, 'You'll not drop off now, Rufey. We have to get back. Are you remembering the route?'

'Not at present.'

'I hope we haven't much further to go.'

'Can't you think of anything else? Like finding that, if you take a piece, just a very small piece, of this country, you can make it resemble a part of the dales?'

'Can you, now? I wouldn't know.'

'If you try hard enough, allowing for the fact that the dale is mainly pasture and the moors and fells are higher than these so-called hills. You know that.'

'I don't go in for much travelling about.' The truth was, I never took a train into the dales.

'You'd have to get your foot into better trim.'

I judged that at any moment he might drop off, into a dream of his home. We all did, and I reckoned it would have to wait.

Rigby had come to another torn page. This time, the piece that had been hidden under the cape matched the tear. Pleased, he read it.

To keep him awake, I asked him if there was a bit of his dale that looked anything like where we were sitting.

'That stream could serve for the gill I'm thinking of, and though these are sycamores, not beeches, they make similar patterns of shade on the grass. The house down there could be the one I know, and if I let my eyes slip out of focus I can make someone come through its door to meet me.' He paused, then continued, 'But when she does, she won't be tripped by barbed wire, and she won't be made unhappy by the sight of a gun emplacement. The spinney I have in mind doesn't have one of those. It's peaceful and private, *with no risk of being interrupted, Gilbert.*'

I did not enquire about the girl; I had a notion who he was referring to; we'd already had words, a bit sharp, on the subject.

For a long time, watching the shadows of leaves shift to and fro on the ground, Rigby sat with the scrap of paper curled in his palm. Then he took up his grandfather's cape and went back to the deserted offices. There he restored the paper to its nest, certain that he was doing what Gilbert would have wished. Then he strode out of High Wood, through the fields that the sheep had strayed in, along the lane past the quarry he had visited the previous day, crossed the main road, and at last he came to Bonniwell's farm.

Ten

His bicycle was balanced on its seat and handlebars; the back tyre was off. 'Mending a slow puncture,' Liz greeted him.

'You shouldn't!'

'I don't know how you manage to ride it.'

She had polished the wheel. Those of her own cycle were scaled with dried dung that was reinforced with bristles of straw. 'I'm waiting till they've collected enough muck to be put in an exhibition,' she told him. 'I mean, they've not only got the visuals; there's the pong as well.'

'Not as strong as that sheep behind the building in High Wood.'

'Is that what's making the stink? I was up there last month.' She did not say why, or whether anyone had accompanied her. 'So the cape is Mr Miller's.'

'I hadn't realised I'd brought it with me.'

Liz raised an eyebrow. 'You must have had a heavy day.'

'It's been . . .' The only word he could think of was, 'emotional', so he finished with: 'a trial.'

'But it looks as though Mr Miller had a shelter last night, even if it was leaky. He might have come back home this afternoon without me seeing.'

'I don't expect so.' At every stop Gilbert was ahead of him. 'But I have to check. Then I'll take the bike and have another look round.' He visualised the map, saw the two ringed areas that remained unexplored. 'I'll probably start at Great Fell.'

'I'd say it's too late now.'

'I suppose you're right.' For the afternoon was passing. Soon it would be twilight and to search would be impossible. He thought of the previous time Gilbert had disappeared: the police, the helicopter, Gilbert at last running into its probing beam.

'Don't worry, you'll find him, bound to,' Liz encouraged. 'Do your mum and dad know he's gone?'

'Not yet.'

She nodded. 'I can see why you have to be quick. You haven't forgotten my telephone number?'

He recited it. 'I'll have to go. Only, do you have an atlas at home, Liz, that I could borrow?'

'Yes. Dad's bought a new one recently. I was with him. He said to the assistant, "Now I don't want one of those all coloured in with pink. We've done with the empire. My interest is in the distribution of beasts in the EU." I had to go out, got the giggles.'

When she had fetched the atlas, she said, 'The scale's minute. Wouldn't a road atlas be better?'

'It's Normandy I want.' Coming from High Wood it had struck him that the pencilled figures in the margin of Gilbert's map could denote latitudes, but not English. He had been appalled that this had not occurred to him before.

Liz was staring. 'Normandy? Are you planning a holiday?'

'No.'

'Then you could be losing your grip. Better get these down you. They're just out of the oven.' She handed him a paper bag. There was a smell of pastry and meat.

'You've saved my life. Are you sure?'

'That I want to save your life? I'll think about it. Mum's making pasties for the men's dinners next week. She'd have no probs feeding the five thousand *without* the miracle. And she's had this in the fridge all day. It's Mr Miller's.' Liz gave him a bottle of milk.

They would bring jugs of milk, and bread straight out of the oven that tasted sweeter than any I've had before or since.

'Thanks,' he said.

'Any time. And Rig, I've been thinking. About Henry Watkins. He didn't admit he hasn't been invited to Heather Dale's party, so obviously he would like to be.'

'I don't think that follows.'

'It doesn't, exactly; and the party's no big deal, is it? But if he would like to go, I could get him a ticket, I'm sure.'

'Why would you do that?'

'I can't say. I'm a puzzle to myself. I mean, why am I servicing this bike?'

Watkins would have found an answer, something on the lines of: Because you are a generous and warm-hearted young lady.

What Rigby did was shrug and say, 'Don't ask me.'

They would line the streets and cheer, and the girls would grab chaps and hug them and kiss them, notwithstanding the muck and the sweat.

The Cornish pasty was delicious. He resisted the temptation on the path to the house but succumbed as soon as he reached the porch. Then he was faced with the choice of eating the second one or saving it. Good sense won and, having allowed himself a small nibble of the wavy crust, he returned the pasty to the bag.

The key was still wedged under the water butt; nobody had been in the house that day.

So Gilbert was still roaming. Somewhere beyond this gill, in the valley, or up on the moors. Concealed by darkness that was moving in fast. Did that please him? Rigby asked himself, suddenly angry. Did he settle in some gully, in some abandoned shippon, in the draughty shelter of some wall? And cackle at his cleverness, jubilant, recite to himself: 'They'll not find me here.' But Rigby's frustration soon receded. It retired before the picture of another Gilbert: conscripted to fight, young, frightened, capable of unenvying admiration, always longing for companionship.

And his grandfather was not playing hide and seek; he had a more serious purpose.

He opened Mr Bonniwell's atlas at northern France and laid it on the table. The latitude on the coast of Normandy was approximately 40°20'. He compared this with the numbers Gilbert had written in the margin of his map. Roughly in line with the rings, they ranged between 49°20' and 49°10'. This small distance was a measure of the slow, arduous advance of the English troops. Though certain that his hunch had been correct, that these numbers denoted latitudes and had no connection with horse racing and betting odds, Rigby could not guess why Gilbert had put Epsom. It was opposite one of the areas he had yet to locate.

He had resorted to holding the map near the lamp to see whether a word had been rubbed out but the lead pencil had left an impression, when the telephone rang.

'Had any joy?' Ben asked.

'I haven't seen him but I know where he's been.' He went through his day, beginning with the missing cape and the report of the man who had stayed at the farm, then describing his search for the places marked on the map and what he had found.

'I'm astonished. I didn't imagine you would come across anything like that. Hang on a moment, let me close the cupboard under the sink; George looks as if he has ambitions.'

'So, one calamity avoided,' he resumed. 'Rigby, I don't want you to feel insulted; it's no reflection on you when I say that I've been having second thoughts. I'm not sure we made the right decision not to tell Mother.'

'I am.'

'She could be hurt that we kept her in the dark, took it into our own hands when she would have wished to deal with it.'

'That's why we did.'

Ben laughed, but briefly. 'I think I'd have to agree with her.'

'Ben, you're not going over to her side?'

'I'm teetering. How long has Grandfather been away now? Thirty-six hours?'

'About that. Carol came to see him yesterday morning.'

'That's a long time for a fellow his age, especially in this season. Look, I'm not happy about saying this when you've done all the work . . .'

'Are you talking prizes?'

'. . . but I really will have to give Mother a ring.'

'I haven't finished looking.'

'We don't know whether anything has happened to him, or the state he's in.'

'He's got plenty of stamina, must have covered as many miles as Watkins.'

'Watkins?'

'He's doing a route-march. We ought to let Grandfather finish his job. He may already have done, but I shan't know till I've found the other places he has ringed. If I do. All of them are connected with the account he wrote for a doctor last time he was in hospital.'

'Hang on. I'm way behind.'

Rigby explained the discovery of Gilbert's narrative and something of what it covered. 'I shouldn't be reading it.'

'It's not necessary to tell me any more. I've got the

gist.' There were small clopping noises made by a tongue against the roof of a mouth. Ben was thinking.

Amazed to hear himself, Rigby pleaded, 'We can't have him pulled in now.'

'I'm with you, but when the chips are down, I shall have to admit to taking the risk.'

'OK. Tell Mother, then,' he flared. 'But I happen to know where to look and I shan't let on.'

There was silence, not even the sound of thinking. Then Ben said, 'I don't suppose search parties could go out tonight. Apart from the logistics, fog is forecast. So I'll make a deal. I'll do nothing before tomorrow. Nightingale will be home later this evening so I'll be able to join you in the morning. Would you object to that?'

'No.' He was obliged to make the concession.

'Have you any idea where you might be?'

Rigby closed his eyes, considered the ground. He would begin with Epsom. He said, 'I know where I'll be going first thing, but if he's not there I'll have to comb Great Fell.' Comb! Rake would be better. With a harrow. A harrowing job. He winced at the pun.

'I'll make sure I've a full tank of petrol. We'll give him to midday.' Ben's voice changed. 'Oh, no! The Scion's been frisking the rubbish bin. He's chewing something. How do I make him spit it out?'

'Enjoy a snack, George,' Rigby shouted, but he had been cut off.

This evening Ben had not invited him to stay in his house, and Rigby was relieved. He did not have to go through the business of declining, of trumping up weak excuses. He was very tired; he had slept badly and got up early; after handing over his cycle, he had had a long tramp. But this was not the most urgent reason for preferring to be alone; he wanted to sort out the chaos in his head, the strange dim intimations that he had to bring into the light.

He stared at the line of coast that was so short in the atlas, where men frightened and seasick had been landed to wade through mines and into the defending bullets and shells. Somewhere within the latitudes Gilbert had recorded there had been the site of an abbey or a church; in its rubble and dust a nun's beads had been found. Somewhere there had been an abandoned farmhouse, its floors splashed with the blood of two opposing soldiers, its barn sheltering their bodies among the scratching hens. In a spinney too small to be depicted in the pages of an atlas was a stream and a gun position that had looked down on a shelled house. To represent this place, his grandfather had sought out a wood where beeches concealed offices that had been assembled in the last war. He had chosen well.

And on a sturdy, out-of-print edition of his English map, Gilbert had recreated two other places. What had happened there? Perhaps that would be described in the last section of his account.

Rigby laid it on the table and turned the pages.

Eleven

Rufe fell silent and although I was no countryman – a walk in the park being the nearest I ever got to sampling grass – I told him I liked how he had described that bit of the dales. The spinney sounded nice, quiet, and I wouldn't mind a slice of that myself. He opened his eyes and regarded me, and for a moment the strain had gone out of his face.

'You're making a big drama out of that foot,' he scolded, but not harshly. 'You might find the going easier without your pack. I'll take it.'

I objected, of course, but not enough to make it final, he was already adjusting the straps. When he had got it rigged on top of his, Rufe fished a bottle of Stupor Juice out of a pocket. 'We'll drink to the Dales,' he said, yanking out the cork. 'Which are, by the grace of God, a million miles away from Leeds.'

I didn't feel strongly enough about my home town to be insulted, especially after taking a swig. But I did feel put out after I had thanked him for carrying my pack and all he could answer was: 'Strikes me I haven't a choice, Whiner.'

'No! I did not say that!' Rigby gasped. The words pulsed in the room's silence, making him flinch. He thought: What is this story doing to me? Then stated, his tone defensive, 'But if I had called him Whiner, Watkins would have deserved it.'

I do not know whether you understand what Stupor Juice was, Doctor, and I do not mind explaining, but I have given out a hint about a young lady and I think I ought to say a word or two about her first.

It was some weeks before the invasion, before we had been transported to the assembly areas along the south coast. We knew something was coming, rumours were the order of the day, but we did not know where, or when, or what regiments would be sent. A lot of letter writing went on, although not so much as just before embarkation when every man jack of us was scribbling off messages, hoping they would not be the last.

I was out of barracks one evening visiting the pictures and as I left I caught up with Rufe and this young lady. We got talking. To be honest it was me and her did the talking. Rufe listened in.

I asked if she had liked the picture, it was *In Which We Serve* and she said she had, but Rufe had not been keen, 'Were you, Rufe?' He made no comment, only shook his head.

The young lady and me exchanged views on the picture, talking about bits we most liked and so forth. I had the feeling that if she hadn't been taken up for the evening with Rufe, I would have been in with a chance, she being a friendly young lady with plenty about her, quite a personality, I thought. She kept trying to bring Rufe into the conversation but he was surly and answering short. I asked her if she lived in the town and she said, No, she was visiting, which fetched a grin from Rufe. I did not like to enquire where she came from, not wanting to look too forward, and since I had no more topics of conversation up my sleeve and Rufe was impatient, in the end I said I had to be back in barracks. I held out my hand with, 'I'm pleased to have met you . . .' pausing, not knowing her name.

She took this up, flirting a bit, but not in any brash way. 'Have a guess. I'll give you a clue: my mother likes flowers.'

Now flowers are not my strong point, but I tried with 'Iris?' and she shook her head.

I had a few more gos, like Lily, and Pansy, and Hazel, and after each one she said, 'No.'

I came to a halt with 'Daisy' and Rufe, who was laughing by then, suggested Chrysanthemum, to which she demanded, straight, 'What colour?' and he answered, 'Red, always. It will never be yellow, will it?'

Then they had a peculiar exchange, giving each other names of flowers that I had never heard of; they were playing a game but underneath they were serious, coming out with the names as if their two lives depended on it. I was flummoxed, but I've since discovered what it was all about. They were courting each other, wooing, not by giving flowers but by saying their names, because each one had a meaning, and the pair of them knew what it was. I cannot remember all the flowers they mentioned but I do recall single pink, which I've learnt conveys *pure love*, and celandine which stands for *joys to come*. He said, 'American cowslip,' which states *You are my divinity*, and she answered, 'Dwarf sunflower', which stands for *adoration*. When she said, 'Cuckoo pint,' Rufe came in with, 'Wake Robin,' and both mean *ardour*. She laughed when he told her, 'Quince,' that meaning *temptation*, but she was a bit tearful when they got to 'Lotus flower' which signals *estranged love*. Then Rufe said, 'Green locust tree.' Seeing what that did to her, he tried to pass it off with: 'Don't fret, I won't hold you to it,' and with his arm round

133

her, they walked away, leaving me standing on the pavement.

I do not suppose you can appreciate what my feelings were, Doctor. You are not a lady who would be pushed aside, so you will not have had the misfortune to hear a young couple talking in code and not being able to crack it, but knowing for a certainty it is expressing their private feelings. Isn't it called being a gooseberry? It was not the kind of situation I could demand an apology for. The truth was, I had only myself to blame. I had barged in, and on reflection I was surprised at myself. All the same, it took me a while to get over them ignoring me. I had taken a liking for the young lady the minute I saw her.

I am not sure whether I would have been less put out if I had known the message resting in Rufe's last choice: Green locust tree. It was not till years afterwards I discovered what the meaning was, and I saw the occasion in a new light. But by that time I had no more tears to shed.

What Green Locust Tree stands for is: *affection beyond the grave*. I've asked myself many times whether, having his mind cast in that direction, it was the reason Rufe had no patience with interruptions. Anyway, next morning he made his opinion on them very plain when he tracked me down in the canteen.

'Well, thanks very much, Gilbert,' he began, standing by the table. 'I really appreciated your contribution yesterday evening.'

I nodded, ignoring his sarcasm. 'Any time,' I told him. The blokes near us were all ears.

'I wouldn't advise that. I just might fill you in.'

The man sitting next to me put down his eating irons, getting ready.

'In that case, Rufe, I'll give you fair warning when I plan to visit the Plaza again.'

'I resent your interference.'

'I wouldn't call it interference.' Down the table, men were pushing aside trays, tossing back the last drops of tea in their mugs. Muscles and fists were begging to be put to service. It was not a question of siding with one particular party; who went for who would be a simple matter of nearness. 'I was only having a few words.'

'They weren't invited. We had better things to do than talking about pictures.'

Somebody laughed. Another commented, loud, 'Of course you had, Rufe.'

He blushed.

There was a call: 'Gilbert was trying to queer your pitch, was he?'

'But he didn't manage it, did he, Rufe?' someone shouted. 'Else you wouldn't have stayed out all night.'

135

He told the company, 'He's been put on a charge.'

'Didn't want to waste any time, was that it, Rufe?' and 'Raring to go, were you?' and 'Gilbert should have known better,' were other comments.

One said, 'I didn't know you went in for all night stands, Rufe,' which caused laughs. He was popular, was Rufe, although a loner at heart. For me, it worked the other way, being set on company and – I can admit it now – not over-liked. Some are blessed with the gift of getting on easy with people, but by and large it passed me by.

While the men squeezed as much smut out of the situation as they could lay their tongues to, Rufe remained standing, his colour high. He had made a mistake to complain to me in public; he had shown his private feelings. It was the only time I saw him at any kind of disadvantage.

He leant across the table and growled, 'Anyway, you didn't succeed in spoiling things.'

Because I had guessed what they were saying to each other in their code, and by that morning the hurt of being made a gooseberry was less sharp, I answered him, 'I'm glad.'

Rigby became aware that the telephone was ringing and he got up hastily, knocking over his chair. He rushed to the chest of drawers, seized the handset. 'Why, it's you, Rigby!' his mother greeted him. 'Don't you get an eerie feeling when you hear a different voice from the one you are expecting?'

Playing for time, trying to activate talking-with-Mother mode which was going to require a lot of subterfuge, not to say deceit, he answered, 'Whose voice were you expecting?'

'Why, Dad's, of course. I must have pressed the wrong number after the memory button. Three, instead of four.' The former stored Ben's telephone number.

'Easy thing to do.' He thought: I'm not forced to correct her.

'It's very nice of you to say that. I'm so hopeless with present day technology. All these complicated machines.'

He wanted to say: Telephones have been around for over a century, Mum. But he toned that down to, 'It does take a bit of time to get used to them.'

'It's sweet of you to be so encouraging. And, Rigby, you mustn't think I'm disappointed to have caught you and not Dad. Far from it. We haven't seen anything of you since yesterday lunchtime.'

'Watch it, Mum, else you'll soon be confessing that you've missed me.' Grinning, he thought: I bet she won't realise that's a joke.

'Of course I've missed you ... To tell you the truth, I've set a place at table every meal before I've remembered you aren't with us.'

He resisted commenting, I thought people did that when someone was dead; and answered, 'I'm touched.'

'Sometimes, Rigby, I think that you misjudge our feelings for you. Because we don't always see eye to eye with you and don't always agree with your opinions doesn't mean that we don't . . .'

He interrupted to prevent her lurching into emotional diagnosis, 'It a very challenging job bringing up children. I realise that, seeing George.'

'He's a little tyke, isn't he? What's he been up to?' After Rigby had explained, Daphne gave the matter the sort of comprehensive coverage the women in his family went in for.

Sensing that an awkward request was imminent, Rigby told her, 'I'm sorry I can't put Ben on. He's in the bath.'

'Give him my love, then, won't you? And tell him I'm pleased to hear you're managing the babysitting without too many mishaps. All the same, I'm sorry your being at Ben's means you can't come to the choir concert this evening. I expect Carol is disappointed, but I'm sure she understands.'

He had forgotten. Also, he had not rung her. On the

table, among the emptied contents of his pockets, his mobile phone rebuked him. He said, 'Mum, could you please put her on?'

'She's already left, which is a relief. She's been on edge all day.'

But not because of the coming concert, he thought. 'Could you mention that I've been trying to contact her?'

'Of course. How nice of you, Rigby. Considerate.'

He winced. Now to 'mature' had been added 'considerate.' It could not be regarded as an appropriate description of lying.

Daphne said, 'We've ten minutes before Philip and I have to be off so I can give Dad a quick ring. I'll make sure I press the right button this time.'

'I wouldn't ring him if I were you, Mum,' he intervened fast. 'I did at about this time a week or so ago and he was very cross to be fetched out of bed.'

'He hasn't mentioned it, but he wouldn't want to give the impression he was complaining. He is extremely fond of you, Rigby. In fact – I know I should not be saying this – I suspect that you are his favourite grandchild.'

He thought how unfair that would be. Carol was so very fond of him. He recalled Gilbert's sidelong looks as he tried to assess Rigby's reaction to a joke, an opinion, some friendliness.

He was popular, was Rufe, although a loner at heart. For me, it worked the other way, being set on company and – I can admit it now – not over-liked. Some are blessed with the gift of getting on easy with people, but by and large it passed me by.

And he asked, urgent, 'Mum, what's Rufe short for?'

'Why, Rufus, of course.'

'Yes.' He felt stupid at wanting to have the knowledge confirmed.

'Why do you ask?' Her tone had changed, was slightly wary.

'No particular reason.'

'When Dad was in the army, a soldier in his regiment was called Rufus. Like William Rufus, Redbeard, son of William the Conqueror.'

Who had invaded from Normandy. The Norman conquest.

'I think they must have lost touch after Dad was sent home from France.'

'I didn't know that he was.'

'He was badly wounded. That was before he and Mother were married. How they wangled a wedding when he was in hospital, I've no idea.'

'I think I'd better get on, Mother. Clear up George's mess.'

'I'm looking forward to having you back at home,' was Daphne's farewell.

'You're a masochist, Mother,' he told her when he had rung off.

He switched on the electric fire and stood reflecting on this conversation. So far, neither his grandmother nor the marriage had been mentioned in Gilbert's narrative. He could be very reticent when it suited him. Yet he appeared to be telling the doctor so much without reservations, being more frank and personal than Rigby had heard him. He recalled Ben saying, 'If anyone could pull the wool over the psychologists' eyes, it was Grandad.'

There was a smell of scorched denim. Rigby returned to the table. After Gilbert had been wounded, 'they must have lost touch.'

So perhaps his grandfather never discovered what had become of Rufus, or of the girl named after a flower. Rigby was surprised that he found this sad. His own friendships with girls had been brief and awkward. Conversations on a business level that dealt with, for example, homework, exams, general school affairs, games matches, would progress without trouble but small talk brought about instant disintegration. What do you say to a girl who remarks: 'I could kill for Rig's hair'? (The response is definitely *not*: 'To stick on your chin or your chest?') The only girl that talked sense was Liz Bonniwell. He wondered whether she knew the language of flowers. He rather fancied trying out something on that line and toyed with the idea of ringing her, saying, 'Celandine,' to which she might answer – he did not believe in half measures – 'American cowslip.'

He sympathised with his grandfather's listening to a conversation that excluded him. Rigby could imagine him looking left out, hurt.

Yet still hanging on. Incapable of taking a hint. Although he could admit: I had only myself to blame. I had barged in, and on reflection I was surprised at myself. All the same, it took me a while to get over them ignoring me. I had taken a liking for the young lady the minute I saw her.

Rigby tutted, critical yet regretful, and picked up the handwritten sheets.

Yesterday I promised to explain about Stupor Juice, Doctor. I'm afraid it's not a matter redounds to our credit but here goes.

It was early days when I first met it. Our company was holed in not far from what was left of an old windmill and as things were quiet, Rufe said to the lance corporal that if it was all the same with him, he had a small piece of business to see to. Dick laughed and said, 'Blimey, you're a fast one,' meaning Rufe had somehow got an appointment with a local lady, but he detailed me to accompany him as 'another gun if he meets trouble'. I could see that Rufe was not pleased with the arrangement but there was no gainsaying it, so off we went.

When we were out of sight he said, 'You could wait here. You don't have to come all the way.'

'I'm obeying an order,' I told him.

'You're a great one for that, Gilbert. Haven't you learnt that rules are made for bending? Which includes army orders.'

I was not provoked to try it. In any case, I was curious to see what Rufe was about.

'I'm investigating a tip-off,' he explained and when I asked where it came from he said a dispatch rider. He had only to go into a hedge to relieve himself and he would come back with the latest news – what we could expect for nosh if it arrived, what had happened in neighbouring sectors, and the fanciful versions given out by Monty (short for Field Marshal Montgomery).

We tramped along the tracks of tanks that had flattened the yellowing corn till we turned up a slope.

From the top of it we could see a cottage. It had escaped damage of combat but looked uncared for. A shutter hung on one hinge, a gutter was broken, the whitening on the walls was streaked with green damp. Rufe sent out two cooing notes like a dove. A curtain moved at a window.

'What you think you're playing at?' I demanded, getting jittery and holding my rifle at the ready.

'Don't worry,' he answered. 'It's Maquis.' (They were the French resistance fighters, and they supplied a lot of useful information, particularly at the start.)

A young woman appeared in the doorway. Rufe held out his hands, called the notes again. She pointed at me. 'Put that thing up,' he said. I slung the rifle over my shoulder and she beckoned us to advance. (I cannot defend this action. Both of us knew that it could not be excused. If Sergeant Theaker had found out he would have had our guts for garters, as the saying goes.) When we were within a few paces of her, Rufe said, 'You stay here,' and went forward.

I watched him making gestures; she went into the cottage and came back with something wrapped in sacking which she exchanged for coins. Rufe waved me up and introduced us. He did it in French, mainly, and it was a better species of the language than mine. Our teacher in top class, being an optimist, had made a jab at teaching us a few words but not many had stuck. All the same, I got the drift when he said, 'Vous êtes charmante, M'moiselle,' and that she had made us 'heureux.' I was not over happy myself, but I did not argue the point. They jabbered on for a while, then Rufe sang out 'Vive la France' and she answered with something that he translated as Down with the Boche.

'What's that you've got?' I asked as soon as we had put the cottage behind us.

'Calvados. The local tipple.' He tugged out the cork and handed the bottle to me, saying, 'After you.'

I am no judge of liqueurs and instead of taking a sip or two I had a real swig. It hit me like a burst from a Panther.

'OK?' he asked.

All I could do was nod and watch him have a more moderate taste. 'Mixed with wine or cider, they're calling it Stupor Juice,' he told me. 'Good stuff before going into assault.'

'You should never mix your drinks,' I advised him like a professional toper. The Calvados was taking effect. Rufe merely told me to watch my steps.

'I can't be expected to walk dainty in these boots,' I argued. 'I don't own a pair of shoes like that pretty ma'moiselle. Not surprised she was proud of them.'

145

She had shown them off, even given them loving strokes, talking sixty to the dozen. I had not understood a word.

But it seemed Rufe had. He said, 'The shoes belonged to a collaborator this morning.' (By collaborator is meant a Norman that allied himself with the Germans, for one reason or another.) 'Some of the resistance workers have been settling scores.' Then he exclaimed, 'I've only now realised. I didn't put the two together,' and he rattled on at such a rate that I could not keep up, but what it seemed to boil down to was: Rufe had not understood all the young woman had said at the time, but now he was making some sense of it, and it was to do with reprisals. (Don't forget, Doctor, what bit of my brain not evaporated by Calvados was having to concentrate on where I placed my leading foot.) Following the tone of Rufe's voice I managed comments like, 'That's not nice,' and 'Who would have thought it?' and 'You're right, there, Rufe,' but that was my limit.

Rigby paused, amazed by this description of a drunken Gilbert. It would have been a revelation to the landlord of The Grand Old Duke of York who had grumbled, 'He'll sit here all night over half a glass of bitter.' Then he asked himself: How many of the troops had a tot of

Stupor Juice before an attack? He did not blame them. He thought he would have done the same. There was a lot about fighting he had never imagined, particularly the less obvious details such as the issue of benzadrine for D-Day and sometimes the shooting of prisoners. When he had told Ben about that, he had said, 'I understand there were incidents. On both sides. Not for us, sitting comfy, to judge.' Rigby was glad that there in a strange country, during a rest from combat, the man Rufe had bought a bottle of Calvados and Gilbert had got legless. 'I'll have to tell him,' he said aloud, then thought: When?

I became a little more eloquent when he stopped to tip the Calvados out of the bottle. I pointed out that I did not approve of waste.

'Haven't you heard me?' he demanded. 'I've bought this from someone who has been settling scores.'

I said I expected there would be scores to settle in the present circumstances. Since I had had a lot of trouble with that, I would not have tried any more but Rufe was waiting, the bottle poised. I managed, 'We don't have the whole picture.'

'We've got enough. I'm sorry, Gilbert, that you haven't more principles.'

I told him I did have one very decided principle which

was: when you have paid for something you don't the next minute throw it away.

'So you can ignore this is booty, the prize of revenge?'

I owned that revenge was nasty but understandable.

'You haven't listened! Revenge is their business. I'm talking about us benefitting from it.' His temper was up and we came near to blows, myself arguing my opinion and him screeching enough to fetch out the 12 ss Panzer division. There was an element of frustration in it, too, since he was not making much progress in pouring out the Calvados, the fruit being stuck like a bung in the neck of the bottle.

'Won't you pay attention?' he yelled. 'I'm telling you this Calvados came from the same place as the shoes. And I bought it. That's as good as saying I approve of what they did.'

I told him that I didn't exactly approve of reprisals but I might take a different line if a collaborator had shopped a friend or one of the family, and I would rather Rufe did not go into what might have happened after.

'You haven't any idea what I'm talking about, have you? I'm telling you that *revenge* is their concern. *Benefitting* from it is mine. And I refuse to do that.'

I saw that he had succeeded in dislodging the fruit in the neck of the bottle. 'Hang on a minute,' I said to him.

All the thinking and debating had made me thirsty. I managed to get in a reminder that we had already compromised our position by trying the goods. In which case, there was nothing lost if we carried out another test.

'By all means, if that's how you see it,' he said, quieter but scornful.

I cannot swear that he joined me but I do have a recollection of him propping the bottle against a tree root. Since no comment was made next morning, I can only deduce that Rufe got me back to our position without mishap. I was grateful he did, and I took good care not to mention that he had disposed of a bottle of Calvados. I noticed that he never concocted Stupor Juice unless he was sure that the ingredients could not contaminate his principles. I respected him for that.

The thing that sticks in my memory, though, is the pair of us nearly putting up our fists over the matter that night. Only not as enemies, as a couple of young chaps wanting to settle an argument. It was heated, but not spiteful. That's how I like to think of us.

Rigby repeated aloud, That's how I like to think of us. It had a final sound. Perhaps Gilbert simply meant that he did not wish to remember their disagreements and Rufe's impatience with his company.

He had nearly reached the end of the narrative; only a few sheets remained. But for the moment he could go no further. **That's how I like to think of us.** The words stayed with him, plain, mournful purlings in the air.

Twelve

Going into the kitchen, Rigby saw the bottle of milk
Liz had handed over, and took a deep draught. It was
such an improvement on what he had drunk earlier
that he would have finished the bottle had he not
warned himself: Better save some for Grandad. Standing
it in the refrigerator, he did not add: If I find him.
He would not allow any doubt; he must find his
grandfather tomorrow, and by midday. He must succeed
before Ben brought in the heavies.

After foraging for biscuits, he fetched Gilbert's
narrative and lay on the sofa, a supine position being
the regular one for most in-house activities: listening to
his music, calling Tim on his mobile, learning lesson
notes, avoiding recruitment for chores, enjoying a
quiet snack. The last left a residue of crumbs and other
small débris over his personal environment but it was
cheerfully accommodated.

He was woken by the clock, nine resounding strikes.

For a moment he was disorientated, unable to explain two red stripes of heat in the hearth that glowed on scattered pages and a cone of light on top of a post. It became a reading lamp above a table humped with documents and carrier bags. He got up, went to the lavatory, closed the bedroom curtains, locked the house door, hung the cycling cape from a hook near the sink. None of these actions interested him; they were to delay. The sight of the written sheets alarmed him. Eventually, scolding himself for this foolishness, asking himself: What are you afraid of reading? he collected them up.

The paper clip that had held the sheets together had vanished. Rigby went to the chest of drawers, lifted out his grandmother's sewing box, found a pin.

'Stand still while I pin this up,' she had ordered. 'See we get the right length.' She was making him a dressing gown, green and soft as moss, and she had lifted him on to the table. 'My, aren't you the bobby dazzler?' she had exclaimed, admiring her work.

'I'm going to take it to school,' he told her, 'and show Mrs Hobhouse.'

'Mind she doesn't filch it. She'd burst the seams trying to get in.'

The idea was so hilarious he had nearly toppled off the table.

'Come and look at yourself,' she had said, and led him upstairs to the long mirror in the bedroom.

Kneeling beside him, she had put an arm round his waist as he preened. Her face was happy, proud. With him, she was always frank and relaxed, tolerant of mischief. She never looked at him askance, checking his reactions. Her speech never bothered him with hints of complications. Rigby had loved her. Holding the pages of her husband's war history, he grieved.

In the sewing box was her needle-case; it was designed as a book. Inside, on the fabric pages neatly serrated by pinking shears, his grandmother had fixed her needles; on the canvas covers she had used bright wools to embroider, in needle-point, Flora Kilshaw. She had made the needle-book before she was married.

He stared at the first name. Although he knew it was his grandmother's, he had rarely heard it. Gilbert had called her My Sweetheart, or Sparrow, and Daphne always addressed her as Mother. He whispered to himself: *Flos*, genitive *floris*, a flower. *Flora*, the goddess of flowers.

I held out my hand with, 'I'm pleased to have met you . . .' pausing, not knowing her name.

She took this up, flirting a bit, but not in any brash way. 'Have a guess. I'll give you a clue: my mother likes flowers.'

He said to himself: Could that woman have been the Flora that Grandfather married? He stroked her name worked into the cover of the needle-case and the ball of his thumb appreciated the soft, vivid wool.

But she had loved Rufus.

Still holding the case, he crossed to the table, sat under the lamp and untied the ribbon round the bundle of letters. He went through them scrutinising the post marks and putting aside those Flora had received after the end of the war. That left a good number, and the address on the envelopes was written in several hands. None was his grandfather's. Three were identical, the writing not laborious, indicating an unaccustomed task, but confident, flowing, giving the impression of speed. Two of these letters had been posted before D-Day, had been slit open with care; the third had no stamp and was unsealed. Inside was a sheet of paper and another folded into a small packet, its end closed by a slender gold pin. Immersed in his desire to identify the sender, Rigby without hesitation pulled them out.

The letter began:

Dear Flora,

I want to talk to you. I want to tell you how I feel for you but I cannot because I'm in the wrong place; you are not sitting beside me. Some of the men succeed in writing down how they feel, but I cannot. If I did, I know that my love for you would show on my face, as theirs does for their girls, and I do not wish anyone else to share it. Therefore I need privacy when I write, and there is none of that here. Someone is sure to butt in, especially one chap, the one you met when we went to the Plaza and rather liked.

Rigby's eyes lingered over *the one you met when we went to the Plaza and rather liked*. Three of them. Flora and Gilbert and . . . Rufus.

This letter had come from Rufus.

There is something I can tell you, though. It is that you keep me sane in the middle of this terrible business. I hoard you and me apart, in another place. I think lots of the men do that. Our place is the spinney above your farm. Whenever I can, I close my eyes and return us there. The others believe that I am contriving to snatch a brief nap, and they remark that is all I need, to be refreshed. But I am not sleeping. It is not sleep that has restored me; it is those minutes with you. I have not been simply remembering them. Often I have been, literally it seems, stretched out with you beside me, and the stench of cordite and smoke and burnt corn and rotting animals has dispersed, leaving in my nostrils the scents of warm grass and your clean, washed skin.

That is how you help me. I find you in our place when I am surrounded by scenes I could never have imagined and that I hope you never have to see. I suppose that is one reason why I'm in this war. I am not only thinking of what happens to the men, but to the land and the villages. So much is destroyed. I am glad you cannot see it. You would weep.

I try to be a good soldier because that way, I tell myself, I shall not make mistakes, and I'll come out of this OK. But that is to connive with deception. Which way the dice fall is a matter of luck. But try not to worry. I would hate you to worry about me who am such a small speck among the millions who suffer in this world.

There was no farewell, no signature.

Rigby laid down the letter, assuring himself that it was a draught that had made it flutter in his hands. And he knew that, like Rufus, he connived with deception.

He wondered why it was left unfinished. Had Rufus received one from Flora that discouraged him from writing more? Rigby thought of her. Affectionate, tender, she had not changed from the girl who had spoken the language of flowers. Yet she had married Gilbert. Loyally, he declared, 'She would not have broken with Rufus just like that! Especially when he was abroad, in the middle of a war.' So perhaps the letter was mislaid, or lost, or he had no opportunity to finish it. Even so, it was here.

But Gilbert's words, That's how I like to think of us, soughed in his head and Rigby had to acknowledge that there could be another explanation.

The telephone was ringing. When he answered it, Ben said,

'Rigby? You sound distant.'

'Normandy is a few hundred miles away.'

'You're still reading about it?'

'Yes.'

'This is a quickie. Carol has news of Gilbert. She gave me a ring during the interval of the choir concert.'

'I think I agreed to go.'

'I couldn't get there, either. I suppose I could have taken George in his carry-cot but I don't think the fellow would have been welcome. Carol's news is, there's been a sighting. Grandfather was seen trying to cross the river by the stepping stones at Hardisty's Lathe. Can you imagine that?'

'I'd rather not.'

'He had his spade to help him, but when he realised he was watched, he began to totter. Apparently Gilbert yelled at the onlooker to keep away, that he had got as far as this and he had no plans to surrender, and if the chap fired, then it would be a cowardly action to shoot a man in his back when he was making a strategic withdrawal. He did drop into the river but managed to stay upright, which was an achievement considering the state of the river bed. Along that stretch it's a mess of stones and lumps of rock and I can vouch they're slippery as ice. The water was past Gilbert's knees but somehow he reached the bank and scrambled off. Hardisty's Lathe is only a few miles from Great Fell.'

'He'll be there by now.'

'No, Rigby, you mustn't consider that,' Ben interpreted his thoughs.

'His trousers are soaked.'

'I've taken that in! But looking for him tonight won't dry him out. There's not even a splinter of moon, and the forecast was right: there's fog about. What's it like your end?'

'I haven't looked.'

'He could be two steps away and you wouldn't see him. You'd need the sense of smell of a dog.'

'I could take a torch.'

'For heaven's sake, Rigby! Do you think you could light up that fell with a few sweeps of a flash lamp?'

He accepted Ben's reasoning but he wanted to hear the arguments for searching that night contradicted, not because he feared the dark but because it made a hunt futile.

'I might find him.'

'I wouldn't like to calculate the odds.'

'There would be no danger.'

'Certainly that fell isn't riddled with potholes or old mine shafts, but if he were to hear you, Gilbert might be frightened and do something . . .'

'Like?'

'I don't know. But according to the account of the young lad who saw him at the stepping stones, Grandfather was not behaving very rationally, was he? This boy told Carol that he thought it was the sight of his combat fatigues and rucksack that caused the trouble.'

'Well, he would say that. Watkins is mad about his kit.'

'You mentioned this Watkins earlier. He seems to get around.'

'Too much.'

'Ah. Carol didn't know his name, but she said he's in your form. Apparently not bad looking, clear complexion, nice manners, and not at all scruffy. Obviously extremely personable.'

He knew Ben was teasing him but he could not prevent the answer: 'She's got rotten taste.'

'Like that, is it?' Then Ben's amusement faded. 'I have to get supper for Nightingale, she's due home any minute. So I'll see you tomorrow as planned.'

'Yes.'

'And you'll not try to look for him tonight?'

'No.'

Rigby folded the letter. 'Why didn't you sign this?' he asked the sender. He stared at the small packet that accompanied it. If I open that, he told himself, my question will be answered and I don't want it to be, not yet. The idea embarrassed him. He hated it when anyone claimed to have had a premonition and went on to describe it with a showy, awe-stricken drama. Yet this evening he could not ignore the alarm that the little packet provoked.

So he left it by the letter and returned to his grandfather's narrative.

. . . the pair of us nearly putting up our fists over the matter that night. Only, not as enemies, as a couple of young chaps wanting to settle an argument. It was heated, but not spiteful. That's how I like to think of us.

It strikes me, Doctor, that with all this talk of ladies and Stupor Juice you'll be thinking that I've gone off the subject of fighting a war, but it's not so easy denied. The trouble is, it gets so it's the normal thing. There are sights and sounds that bring you out in a sweat like they did first off, only you've learnt how to keep yourself in hand. And another thing while we're at it, there's a lot of time wasted. In other words, time when you're kicking your heels. You can hang about hours waiting for the order to commence an offensive, and then there'll be news it's postponed, or you can start out and before you've reached assault area you're withdrawn, not a shot fired. Strategy can be decided, plans can be made, but that doesn't take account of hitches or what ruse the enemy's hit upon, requiring a change of commands. The Germans were good at adopting new tactics to fit altered conditions, being especially quick off the mark when it came to mounting a counter attack. We used to grumble when we were messed about (not the word we gave to it) but that was not so surprising when you know, only we did not at the time, that it was not long before over a million Allied forces had been landed in Normandy, not forgetting the armour, stores, food, kitchens, medicals and such like, and that's a number takes some organising.

When it comes to outright engagements you would have been hard pressed to make much sense of what went on if you had been asked to cook up a report the next day. There's one battle that stands out, though, and not because it went like clockwork, it did no such thing, and not because we had a clear sight of what was going on. There was a time during it when we saw nothing from start to finish. Eyes were useless. We fought by feel.

It was near the end of June and our division was taking part in a big offensive, Monty having come up with a strategy to encircle Caen. According to the papers back home, we had reached Caen by D-Day, only we had not, any more than we did on this occasion. The offensive was called Epsom.

'That's one puzzle solved,' Rigby said to himself, recalling the name his grandfather had written on the map; 'and the area inside the circle must commemorate where this offensive took place.'

We had already been on the alert but nothing had come of it, the reason being, according to reports, that supplies had been held up by a gale in the Channel. We were sceptical about this but later we learnt that it wasn't a piece of eye-wash come down from HQ but a fact, the worst gale in the Channel for forty years. Weather does not take account of military planning. None of us liked the delay. When there is a battle in the offing you want to get on with it, know one way or the other how you are placed. Marking time does no good to the nerves and it takes men different ways: some go quiet and look as if they are practising being dead (not my joke, Doctor; I repeat the phrase to give you the idea); some get all busy and bull up their rifles like they are intent on making a smart entry through the pearly gates (another one by the same comic; it earned him a warning said in no uncertain language which he had the sense not to ignore). Some brew up every five minutes, some like me pace about trying to start distracting conversations and Rufe sits with a pad on his lap and writes letters.

I found a patch of earth that still had a few whiskers of grass in it and sat down not far from him.

He looked up and asked, 'Do you want anything, Gilbert?'

'I'd like to get started.'

'That won't be till early morning. I've got it on good authority. Zero hour's 04.15 hours and I'd like to finish this first.'

'I'll leave you to it, then,' I told him.

He said, 'I'd appreciate that,' and I was glad for once I'd done the right thing.

Not long after, we mustered. There was no sign of dawn and the air had an edge to it. Rufe, who was alongside me, remarked, 'It's got an autumn feel.' I was less interested in the season, true or false, than I was in the coming assault. Sergeant Theaker had given us the run down of what armour was being deployed and our objective and it seemed we were in the thick of it. Anyway, there was no need for a regular dawn, the artillery was providing a replacement, stuff flashing in the sky, never a moment's pause, tracers, explosions from our heavies and shells from cannons on ships that were lying off the coast miles away. It has always been a puzzle to me how anything, man or mouse, can survive bombardments like that, but they do and rear up ready for the fight. They did that day, as soon as we reached them.

When we got the order to move, our gunners behind began laying a creeping barrage. That's a carpet of fire put down ahead of you and preceding you as you advance, the intention being to reduce the opposition. It's a practice not without danger. You can be shot in the back with a round made in Britain if there's been a miscalculation. That day, though, there were no mistakes.

I did not hear any noise from our men as we paced forward but that was nothing to go by since they could have been shrieking like banshees or sobbing like lunatics, I would not have heard them, the noise above and in front blocking my ears. We were moving down a gentle hill into standing corn, not seeing that very clearly because of the muck raised by the barrage, but I was surprised to get a view of the tops of trees that were below our sight line. It was as if they were expanding then shrinking to nothing as the light of shell-bursts switched them on and off. One was hit and it erupted, tatters of it spurting into the air then flopping down, except for a few that stayed up and floated away. Rufe shouted, 'Look at the rooks!' I heard him because the noise had slackened a bit, which was always a fearful sign, like a preying creature being very still, waiting to pounce. That day the pouncing was done by enemy infantry, but before we reached them we found ourselves in mist.

Mist is not the right word, though no doubt that is how it began. It was a thick, choking porridge of fog, smoke, fumes, muck from our barrage and the enemy's mortars, with lumps of wheat ears and stalks floating in it for good measure. As soon as it wrapped round us, we were like men half blinded. We could not see further than an arm's length in front. So we weren't slow to lose direction, with not a landmark to tell whether we were going forward or back in own tracks, let alone whether we were walking straight. We called to one another, tried to maintain contact, but Lieutenant Crosby shouting 'Keep to the right,' was no help if you were facing another way or, for that matter, if he himself was going round in circles. I don't suppose this lasted more than a few minutes before it came to us that some of the voices were not ours. Someone shrieked, 'There's Jerry,' and the next thing was, we were in the position of hand-to-hand fighting.

It is a nasty business, hand-to-hand fighting, and that day it struck me that a lot of war has grown detached from those aimed at. The RAF do not see people they are dropping bombs on any more than a gunner looks his target in the eye when he fires a 25 pounder, and though you see men, the enemy as well as ours, maimed and screwed up with the agony, you do not generally have to watch a body sag and the blood spurt while it is pinned on your own bayonet. That's what hand-to-hand fighting is about; it's not throwing a grenade into a trench and seeing it blow up the contents; it's not hurrying chaps along at the point of your rifle, taking them prisoner. It is being close, right up to a man, feeling the brush of his sleeve, the scratch of a buckle, and the draught of him as he leans in to make his jab. Because of the fog I have spoken of, I did not see the features till the last second, as the face looked up or slid down, then my eyes would take in, but not my brain straight away, the purple fold of tiredness under an eye, the hairs in a nostril dirtied with soot, the pimple on the chin of a lad younger than myself. At such moments it is not your enemy you are putting paid to, it's a man with a photo of his girl in his pocket, who has a history of family and school and work just as you have, who shares your weariness and is as frightened as you. But when the next one crashes into you, you draw back your arm, swing through with your bloodied bayonet, and drive it in.

I had no pride in my success, staying alive, but in one matter I am forever grateful. I did not kill any of our own men. Some were done in that way, it was witnessed, but nothing was said, official. The fog bred panic and in places it was so dense, it was impossible to make distinctions.

I cannot tell you how long we were in that state. The time that passed on the clock had no connection with the time in our heads. It was as if we were held up in another world, and I felt that years were added to the age stated on my papers.

When we came out of the cornfield we seemed to have the upper hand of the enemy so we could make for the village which we were trying to take but, despite the fog lifting, we succeeded in occupying only half of it. So we were not entirely successful, although another company managed to establish themselves on a ridge not far off. That night ours was dug in alongside a muddy stream, and we were on stand-to, there being a lot of enemy activity (shelling) in the locality.

I said to Rufe, 'I'm pleased that fog didn't stay longer.' When he did not respond, I added, 'It was a nasty business.'

'I got the answer to my questions, though. Did you, Gilbert?'

'What questions?' I knew, of course.

He sighed, 'I don't ask many. They came up over the German officer I shot in the farmhouse: Did I do it because I wanted to, wanted to kill? Or did I do it because I didn't want to be killed?'

'I wouldn't have thought there was any doubt about it.'

'You haven't any doubts yourself?'

'You bet I haven't.'

I heard his breath click in his throat. 'I wish I could be as sure. There were moments . . .'

'We weren't ourselves, Rufe,' I interrupted, arguing as if I was talking to a younger brother who had not yet learnt the world's ways.

'I don't know what you mean.'

'The situation took over.'

'That's the usual excuse.'

'This is war. You can't blame yourself every time you kill someone.'

'You've missed my point.'

I had not, but I let that rest.

A little later that night I said, 'I have to thank you, Rufe, for a warning.'

'Have you?' He was not interested.

Punching through the fog had come the shout: 'Gil!' I had swung round, and this had broken an assailant's aim; I heard the rip of khaki as his knife sliced down my sleeve. Off balance, he could not parry my thrust.

'It was your voice,' I told Rufe.

'I think I did a lot of shouting.'

'Then you were helping to stop men from getting it.'

'It was instinctive.'

I persisted. 'Rufe, what I'm saying is, doing that is cause for congratulation, no matter what you suspect you thought when we were fighting in that fog.'

He was minutes before answering. 'My conscience isn't so easily silenced, Gil,' he said. 'But thank you for trying.'

To this day I treasure those words.

Then Gilbert had written:

Not long after that, I was wounded and sent home. The rest of the war was spent at Regimental headquarters doing an office job. I was not sorry for the change.

Underneath was a neat ruled line drawn with a red ball

point pen. Rigby stared at it. How could his grandfather stop there? He imagined Gilbert saying to himself, 'I was told to write about my service in Normandy, and I have. What came after is not wanted.'

'That's not right, and you know it,' Rigby answered him, angry. 'You've admitted how you felt and how you behaved; you've done a lot of confiding, but then, just like you – the way you'll make some remark, a hint, and then not finish – you've clammed up, dropped the shutters. You've started questions like: How did you come to marry Grandmother? and: Did you keep in touch with Rufus? and you haven't turned up the answers.'

There was to be nothing more about this mismatched friendship, about the life of fighting soldiers; no more about Rufe.

Impatient, Rigby left the table. He was hungry and, fetching the second Cornish pasty, he set to work. But eating it too fast, he had no enjoyment. The pastry was not chewed but swallowed in chunks, the gravy did not linger on his tongue to be slowly savoured but was sucked unappreciated down his throat. Because all the time, from his position by the hearth he could see the ruled, red line.

Forget it, he advised himself, set the alarm, be out of the house by five. (Who says he is a late riser?) It would still be dark but he had lamps on his cycle. By dawn he would be able to resume his search.

Beside Gilbert's narrative he could see his mobile phone and he read again Carol's message: Nuz Plez. C. Sorry to have ignored it for so long, he dialled her number.

Thirteen

'Rigby! Hi!' Carol answered. 'I've only just got back.'

He was abruptly bewildered. Beyond this table covered with Gilbert's mementos and his written pages were people spending a normal Saturday evening, at clubs, gymnasia, discos. With friends. Some were returning from a choir concert. He managed the question: 'How did it go?'

'Great! The audience wouldn't stop clapping. Then the Chairman of Governors made a speech. You know, about the value of working as a team and no matter how much talent you have, it's no good without a massive dose of hard graft, effort, diligence etc.'

'I can imagine.'

'He didn't go on for long. Somebody began to clap again before he had finished and Miss Hargreaves at the piano signalled an encore. Mum cried.'

'So what's new? Where is she at the moment?'

Immediately alert to his warning, she answered,

'Downstairs preparing some supper. I'm famished. I'm in my bedroom.'

'Ben's called, told me your news.'

'I didn't know you weren't at his place. I hadn't much time, when I phoned, it was very gabbled. I've felt awful, Rigby, not being able to give you a hand. We had another rehearsal this morning and all I had time for this afternoon was buying out the newsagent; he thought I was off my trolley. I got every local paper including the *Bradford Telegraph and Argus* but there was no mention anywhere of someone being picked up or found. I kept my radio on, switching round the local stations, but nothing was reported.'

He wanted to say, I don't need all this guff; but compromised with: 'How did you come across Watkins? He's not supposed to be making his way home till tomorrow.'

'I didn't meet . . . What's his first name?'

'Henry.'

'I didn't meet this Henry in town. It was a piece of sheer luck.'

That was not how Rigby would have described any meeting with Watkins but he did not interrupt.

'I went out to the newsagent's again to buy the *Evening News* and Goff Brewer was there. We started chatting and he said he had seen you near the Lady

Anne's bridge early afternoon and he offered to take me there, cruise round on the off-chance of finding you. He's got a motor bike.'

'And you said, "I can resist everything except temptation." '

'What I said to Goff Brewer is no business of yours,' she snapped, 'but among other things I did point out that I had no more than an hour free before getting ready for the concert. While I was with Goff we saw Henry and he related what I told Ben. Question answered.'

Rarely could Carol be persuaded to such brisk summarising. It showed the extent of her annoyance. Logging for future reference the caution: Never joke with a woman about her choice of chauffeur, Rigby said, 'I'm sorry I wasn't about.' (About! He had been on the move all day.) 'But the stuff you got from Watkins is useful. It gives me a lead.' Not bad, he congratulated himself.

Pacified, she answered, 'Yes. Ben thought so, too. He said that you would know where to begin looking tomorrow.'

'That's right.' He guessed that Ben had not had time to explain his decision on a deadline for the search and he did not mention it either. Carol would learn soon enough.

She said, 'Rigby, something happened after Henry had told me about Grandfather. Of course, he didn't know who it was, but from what he said the old man was definitely Grandad. Henry told us because, I think, the situation had upset him. We had said goodbye and had turned back, Henry was continuing up the lane, when two other bikers shot past and pulled up in front of him. They started to mess about, tugging at Henry's rucksack, asking to see what was in it, grabbing his beret and trying to stretch it over a helmet, plucking at his combat jacket, wanting him to show them what he wore underneath and, if it was army issue vest and boxer shorts, they would be gratified if he would model them. Goff intervened, telling this Col and Stewart to cool it. He's a really decent sort.'

'He's a show-off.'

'He's got plenty to show off about, but he hadn't finished before Henry interrupted. He told Col and Stewart that if they didn't move aside and permit him to pass, it would be a case of obstruction and he would make a citizen's arrest.'

'He *what*?'

'Yes! I couldn't believe it. They were revving up, it was deafening, and they were nipping Henry between their front wheels and he was really scared and that's what he said, "If you don't move aside, I shall report you or I'll simply make a citizen's arrest." '

'He's mad.' He could hear Watkins' prim voice calling upon a non-existent respect for legality.

'It started them off, they were mimicking Henry, fooling about, putting their hands up, pretending to turn themselves in, asking Goff to be witness and all that. He played along, humouring them, and it looked as if they had had enough and were on the point of going . . . . Oh, no! Mother's calling. Supper's ready.'

'No comment.'

'I'll ring you back, soon as I can. Tell you the rest. I'm worried, Rigby, I really am. Not only about Grandfather. There's Henry as well.'

'A chap who can threaten a couple of bully boys with a citizen's arrest doesn't need you to worry about him,' Rigby told her as she rang off. Then he laughed, but not derisively, enjoying the incongruity of it: Stewart and Col, suited not in clanging armour but in buttock-hugging leather, helmeted in polished plastic, clamped behind fly-splattered visors, and sitting astride steeds that had engines for muscles and whose rigid farings had replaced harnesses ribboned and fringed. And opposing them – *Watkins*. Laden with gear, kitted out for combat but having neither cannon balls nor cannon, flintlock, halberd, mangonel, spear, lance, axe, cutlass, machete, shell, rifle, entrenching tool, tank, rake or spade. 'And he offers to haul them off their motor bikes and march them to the cooler,' Rigby gasped out, sobbing with laughter. 'I like it. I like it, Watkins.'

At last quietening, he began to prepare for the next day. As he put the pages of Gilbert's narrative in order he came upon the jagged edge of the first torn-off strip. The next page began: **I said, 'It'll not come to that.' I had never felt so mournful.**

What had Grandfather written? Rigby asked himself; and why did he tear it out? Was it that he did not wish the doctor to read it? Or, like the scrap hidden in the derelict offices, it belonged to a particular place? What could Rufus have said? Nothing in his grandfather's narrative answered his questions. He pushed the pages into the card wallet with the other documents and slid Rufus's letter to Flora into the unsealed envelope. The small packet belonged with it. Delicately, he picked it up.

It was about the size of a luggage label. Through its paper, his fingers could feel nothing, then they made out a fine coil. Without considering, dismissing his previous apprehension, he withdrew the gold pin that held it closed, ran a thumb under the folded edges, gently turned back the stiff lappet and a tissue of white silk. Underneath was a ring of hair. Released from confinement, it sprang open, a live thing, stopping his breath. Then it fanned out and curved over the paper, a vibrant fringe.

For it contained the colour of all things russet, of maple leaves in autumn, of paprika and cider, of conkers and an Irish setter's coat. As if recently brushed, it shone and glinted, making the gold pin by its side dull and flat.

'It is his,' Rigby whispered. 'His hair. Rufus.'

His mother had said, 'Like William Rufus – Redbeard – son of William the Conqueror.'

With the tip of a finger he stroked the rich tress. It stirred under his touch and he imagined it bordering the band of a soldier's forage cap, curling under the brim of a steel helmet. Disarrayed by the wind, it was groomed by a woman's hand while sun, dropping through leaves, pied it with dazzling light.

Gently, a thumb on the tape that held it, he walked upstairs and stood in front of the mirror in his grandparents' bedroom. The face that looked back at him was not that of a child come to admire himself in a newly made dressing gown and the mirror held no image of a woman kneeling beside him, an arm round his waist. But he remembered the touch of her palm on his nape and the reflection of her mouth, for a moment not smiling but pinched and sad as her fingers crept upwards and combed through his hair. Then he did what he had come to the mirror for. He held the glowing relic of Rufus to his head.

For a long time he stood watching the lamp in the ceiling tease out a soft iridescence, seeing the colour become auburn then deepen to purple as he swayed in and out of the light. Stroking it into his own hair, he saw the two merge; there was no distinction.

'You're throwbacks,' Ben had said about him and George.

Throwbacks, but not very distant. For himself, only two generations away.

Gilbert had known, of course; he had 'wangled a wedding when he was in hospital'. Flora must have been pregnant before the troops embarked for France. Rigby did not linger over this abrupt marriage or the love that it held; he would come to it later. But his grandmother must have told Gilbert that she was carrying Rufus's child. Daphne. Had she been told? Had Ben? Perhaps it was not a joke when he said, 'You're both throwbacks.'

What else had he inherited? Gilbert had written, 'He was thick set, on the heavy side.' To Rigby he had said, 'You've got the frame; it'll not be long before you fill out.' Rigby stood straight and examined himself. He was broad shouldered and his arms were strong looking but his chest had no depth; there was still little sign of

179

pectoral muscles. Grinning, he advised himself, 'I'll have to pump iron.' Then he sobered, feeling disloyal because he had never wished to resemble Gilbert.

A hint of a face formed beside his in the mirror; the mouth smiled but hesitantly. '**Do you want anything, Gilbert?**' Rufus had asked, polite but dismissive. The eyes in the mirror darted to Rigby's, then slipped away. Rufus had passed on more than the colour of his hair and wide shoulders. Aloud, Rigby said, 'I'm sorry, Grandfather,' but the face had gone.

He accused the space it had left, 'The plain fact is, you get up my nose. You can't leave me alone.' *I need privacy when I write . . . Someone is sure to butt in, especially one chap.* 'You can't do anything, or say anything without sneaking a glance to check how I've taken it. You've got a tic, always monitoring my reactions.'

Liz had commented, 'I reckon I know what is Henry's problem; he wants to be liked.'

'Could be,' he answered. 'But it does not explain Grandfather, not entirely. There's more to it than wanting me to like him. Most of the time he acts like we've had an argument and he's in the wrong and is trying to make up. Presenting me with a peace offering. I wish he could behave normally, be straight and come out with what he's got on his mind.'

And he had spent the last thirty hours searching for this man!

It was cold in his grandfather's bedroom; he would warm up if he got under the blankets, but he had no hope of sleep while these people crowded his head. He laid the hair in a palm. For a moment, full of static, strands rose and wafted. This had been sent with the letter that Rufus had not completed. Rigby demanded, 'What happened to him?' He could not say, 'How did the man who bequeathed me his hair genes, die?' Waving back the presences that crowded round him, he descended the stairs.

He laid the tress on the table. Among Gilbert's mementos, it shone up at him, vivid, the inextinguishable flame of a man. Careful not to cover it, he opened the map. He wished to confirm the route to the two remaining locations. Tomorrow he would be searching not only for Gilbert; he now had an additional purpose. In following Gilbert, he would be following the tracks of Rufe.

The telephone began to ring, reminding him of Carol's intention, or threat, to call him again. He looked at his watch: a quarter past eleven. If this were Carol, she must have had a gourmet feast rather than a supper by the amount of time she had taken. He debated whether to answer; she would witter on about Watkins, and he suspected that she enjoyed worrying, it allowed her to express sympathy without the inconvenience of putting herself out. Any positive action could be handed on. To him. As yesterday. If it had not been for Carol, he would not have slogged himself into the ground and be sitting here now in danger of dying through starvation or hypothermia. Glancing at the coil of hair, he admitted, 'Not that I would rather have spent the time at home.' The ringing continued. If Carol wanted to unload her anxieties she must find someone else. On the other hand, the caller might be Liz Bonniwell to tell him that she had misled him; in fact, she has no interest whatever in Watkins except zoological and has changed her mind about offering to procure him an invitation to Heather What's-her-name's party. (And he would definitely *not* remark that he could not work out why so many young women were eager to martyr themselves in the Henry Watkins cause.)

He lifted the handset and shouted, 'Rigby here.'

'I wasn't expecting anyone else,' Carol answered.

Disappointed, he growled, 'It's late.'

'It's about Henry. Do you know he's sleeping out?'

'Yes.'

'It really bothers me.'

'Carol, give over, will you? The dickhead's got a tent.'

182

'Yes, and it caught Stewart and Col's attention, so they started to pluck at it, asking Henry what he intended to do with it, ordering him to erect it because they wanted to try it out. But when they heard Goff's offer to stand them a drink in The Grand Old Duke of York, they stopped. Stewart told him that he owed them one for spoiling a bit of fun and Col told Henry, "You get that tent propped up ready for when we get back and if it flattens under inspection I'll report you to Tawny Owl and she'll put you on a charge."

'After they had gone, I told Henry that all the tent business was an empty threat, their way of keeping up the aggro, and Goff said, "Any brain the louts might have started with has sunk to their mouths." Henry put a good face on it and said nobody on a motor bike would ever reach Withy Syke; and if they did, they wouldn't find him, he would camouflage the tent. Goff remarked he could think of more healthy places to camp than Withy Syke but Henry said it must be OK since his father had made the arrangement. I asked Goff afterwards what he meant and he told me the place is a tip, every piece of rusting machinery from miles round is dumped there and when Tubby Weatherill brought a bull-dozer to shift it, he just made matters worse. Goff also said that Tubby Weatherill only lives at the farm off and on; he has an attachment further up the dale and spends his time with her.'

His eyes on the map before him, Rigby was paying little attention but a name poked through. He demanded, 'Did you say Withy Syke?'

It was printed, insignificant, beside the blue thread of a gill. Nearby was a tiny black building. They lay in the centre of a pencilled ring. He ran a finger across the sheet. In the margin directly in line with the ring was Gilbert's note: Epsom.

'I have to thank you, Rufe, for a warning.'

Punching through the fog had come the shout: 'Gil'. I had swung round, and this had broken an assailant's aim . . . Off balance, he could not parry my thrust.

'It was your voice,' I told Rufe.

To Carol, whose voice was questioning, he said, 'Yes, I'm still here. Do you mind telling me again what Goff said about Withy Syke?'

He did not desire the repetition; he was sparing himself the need to talk. Because while Carol obliged he was pulling on his anorak, stowing his mobile phone in a pocket, collecting the cape. As he did this he discovered that a square of canvas had been taped to the inside of it to provide a rough pocket, and he slid the lock of hair under the flap. Ready, he was careful to wait until Carol had finished, had said her farewells, before he cancelled the call.

At the door, he told himself tiredly, 'Watkins can look after himself; he doesn't need me to be his minder. Stewart and Col's warnings are so much gas, non-combustible, and in any case Mr Weatherill would hear them. Provided he was not with his "attachment." But since I shall be going there early tomorrow, I've nothing to lose by calling in now. I can have a kip in Watkins' delectable tent. If I can find it. If it isn't camouflaged out of existence. He's probably dug it in like a Panther and poked its pole like a 75mm through the *bocage*.'

Fourteen

Outside, the darkness was impenetrable. If there were stars, their light did not pierce through the trees. But the slope down the scythed grass took him to the beck, and the flattened earth under his searching feet gave him the path. At first, he tapped his toes forward before taking a step, testing the ground for hindrances, roots, patches of greasy mud. But soon he had the sense that he was behaving ridiculously and was irked by the snail progress. So, turning, he allowed himself to splash into the water. Once there, he discovered that it gave off a faint hint of light. This was encouraging although it showed him nothing, could not save him from slithering on sunken leaves or tripping over stones on the beck's bed. Yet he kept his balance, was able to increase his speed in water that washed round his ankles. Then deepening, it became unmalleable, obstructing, a force that required effort to part. Therefore he pushed to the edge, took to the path again and resumed his fumbling, hesitant way. But under these trees, by a beck he had played in as a child, there were no beasts or bogies. His concern was haste and the cold, rising wet. At last, when wood snapped round him and scratched his face, he knew that he had walked into a willow that had fallen the previous winter. An unseen landmark, it pointed him to Bonniwell's farm.

A barrier of stone at his shoulder told him that he had reached an outbuilding. He felt along it, came to its end, paused, thought his bearing, and walked without guidance of touch across ribbed concrete, through cow pats and spongy wads of straw. There was a scraping of metal, a brisk shaking, a warning growl. 'Good boy, Albert,' Rigby called, low. 'Nothing to bother about.' Soothed by the familiar voice, the dog snuffled, then was quiet.

His shoes scuffed gravel. Rigby followed its edge until it ended and he stepped upon soft soil. Stretching ahead, his hands flinched at the sting of nettles. Behind them was a wall. At his tap, planks echoed. Walking his fingers down them, he reached the latch of the door, eased it open. Inside, the lamp on his handlebar was the first thing that came under his touch; its promise of light tempted him, but he had to wait. Not until he was through the gate, was out on the road and past the farm, did he switch it on. And not until then, as tarmac and verge appeared out of the darkness did Rigby's breath become even and muscles relax that for the last twenty minutes he had, unknowingly, flexed tight.

When they were choosing the cycle, his father had said, 'These LED lamps are splendid, aren't they? Bright enough to give other road users plenty of warning.' Not inclined to quibble over a gift, Rigby had accepted; later he had bought a lamp that took batteries providing a more powerful beam. He did not intend to restrict his cycling to the town as his father assumed. It was not only a warning light that he was after; he wanted illumination for unlit lanes, unfrequented ways.

Now as the surface of the road rushed towards him, Rigby was released from the dark trough of the beck and the slow, silent creep through the farm. He forgot his soaked denims and trainers and with Gilbert's cape flapping round him he enjoyed the thrust of his feet on the pedals, the strength of his calves, the grip of his fingers on the handlebar. He was king of the highway. There was no noise of an approaching vehicle; there was no sudden flash as a headlight showed round a bend. Taking the long sinuous road to the Lady Anne's bridge, he crossed the ends of tracks to farms but, distant, they were hidden from sight.

Yet gradually, against his good sense and the slant of his personality, Rigby became lonely. Concentrating upon the ground under the beam of his lamp, he was aware that, beyond its fall, the country stretched black, endless. It had no horizon; it was empty of sound, of movement, of breathing life. His satisfaction receded and the task that he had set himself reappeared.

The difficulty weighed on him. He was a fool on a fool's errand, and he could not go back. Because inside a pocket nestled a twist of vibrant hair. Already moving fast he stood on the pedals, pushed harder, and was frustrated by the cycle's imperceptible response.

Though the battery in his lamp was strong, it did not cast a beam very far forward; he had to pick up clues from the appearance of the road's verge. When it led him to the left he realised that he had made a wrong turning; he reversed, suddenly anxious lest he had lost direction. But visualising the map, he saw a small black cross on this part of his route and when he came to a stretch of flags he stopped, swung the lamp. The arc of light found shrubs that grew out of a thin mist, then a chapel, remote and forgotten. He thought: Has Grandfather sheltered here? But against the door a drift of crisp leaves was undisturbed and browned blossoms of spring still clung to a hinge. He continued, crossed the bridge and not long after reached the opening he sought. The gate across it was broken; the name, Withy Syke Farm, hung on a bar. Rigby steered his cycle round and entered a track. It was two deep ruts pocked with holes filled with standing water that concealed bits of rubble, stones, chips of bricks. As he forced his way forward, he noticed that the edge of the ruts were damp where they had taken spray from the puddles; that occasionally on the surface of the water was a dragging spill of oil. But it gave him no clue to the vehicle that had made it, whether a car, a tractor or a van. Or a threatening motor bike.

The track rose for a distance, merged into clinker that ended with a gate; it was warped and unpainted. On each side of it a fine electrified wire was strung between posts, a stay to cattle. He had reached the farm. It was silent. There was no stir of a dog.

Rigby leant his cycle against the fence and unclipped his lamp. With the farm on his right he knew that the stream, Withy Syke, must be ahead of him and within minutes he was on a descending gradient. His lamp confirmed that he was walking through pasture; it was nibbled by sheep and scattered with their droppings. Soon, however, these details became blurred; they were overlaid by steaming gusts like those which had breathed round the chapel. They hazed the glass of his lamp. 'There's fog about,' Ben had said. Rigby carried on. There was nothing else he could do.

For some distance he stepped downwards, then

stumbled as the ground levelled. He switched on the lamp again. It gave no radiance, only an opaque dampness, but at his feet he could make out rusted claws of metal. One tore at his legs and he heard the rip of fabric, felt a point in his flesh. He had come to Mr Weatherill's dump. Pausing, wondering whether he could push through it or should retreat and find a way round, he heard shouts, swearing and menaces; above these was the higher voice of Watkins. Heedless of obstacles, Rigby scrambled towards it.

The fog that had been odourless now carried on its draughts the stench of burning rubber. Rigby's nostrils twitched and he swallowed down coughs, thinking: Better if they don't know I'm here. Already aware of the need for tactics, although he had none, hindered by night and fog. In which the lamp was useless. He switched it off and immediately the darkness was floored by snares. Pipes rolled under him; sand oozing from sacks brought him down. A voice snarled, 'Got you now, Prof,' and a door of a van swung, banged into his side. Near him Watkins answered, 'Keep off!'

After that, the night heaved with bodies. Rigby had to fight by quick recognition of pieces, never the whole. For the fog did not part; it did not thin to reveal figures but thickened, was swollen by some mass that had a chest, arms, tripping legs. Hands came out, tugged at clothing, leaped to a face. A punch found a stomach, was followed by a gasp, the slip of boots on a sheet of plastic. A fist expanded by a padded mitten hit a shoulder, there was a thump, then duck boards cascaded, slithered, wedged between wrecks to form a new barrier. And these feints, blows and misses were accompanied by the tinkling of wire, the echo of feet upon collapsed palings, the thud of flesh against metal, the splintering of glass. And the shouts: 'Col, you keep the fire going'; and Watkins's threat, 'If you burn that, I'll . . .'; and Col yelling, 'This here's a maniac, Stew.'

Rigby seemed to be circling, passing through eddies of smoke. It came from rubber and he halted, choking on the fumes, saw, momentarily, hands converge on his stomach, flex. And before he could defend himself, he was curled against the half-buried wheel of a tractor, retching for breath.

'How's that then, Col?' Stewart rocked a boot on Rigby's throbbing ribs.

'What you been at?'

'Hear him, Prof? We've been having a good natter, of course, haven't we? Shall we show him the bruises?'

'He's been leading me a dance,' Col told him.

'Isn't he a misery, Prof? Never stops bellyaching. But he'll let up soon as he sees that tent burning, won't you, Col?'

'It'll make a nice blaze.'

'You stick your boot on him, then, while I liven up the fire.'

The flame of a cigarette lighter shot up and showed tyres smouldering. Stewart took a newspaper out of a pocket, tore it down the folds and pushed the sheets into the warm ash. A spark settled, took hold and as light spurted, Col said, 'Where's his combat gear, then?'

'Me and him's done a swap.'

'Wrap up, Stew! Take a look.'

But before they had turned him over Rigby realised their mistake. 'Watkins,' he yelled, 'Keep away. Clear off!' Then he was on his feet, was kicking at the tyres, was grinding his boots into the scorched and glowing paper, was hitting out at bulks pressing upon him, was clawing at gripping fingers. Until he was knocked down by a weight that consisted of knees, elbows, fists, and heard Stewart pant, 'You shouldn't have done that, Rigby, lad. I'm saying, you shouldn't have done that.'

But another voice silenced him. Loud and firm it penetrated the fog like a steamboat's hooter and announced, 'I have telephoned the police and given them your exact location. I also reported there is a danger of fire.'

'You heard that?' Col said, whispering.

'I made out a faint yodelling.'

'Boy Scout's phoned the fuzz.'

'They'll have trouble with the morse.'

'Give over, Stew! They're on their way.'

'I didn't hear anything about them being on their way. Hold his feet down, will you?'

'Stew, we've got to move.'

'Rip off his trainers. Now, that's an idea. If we strip him down, he'll be really incommoded in this lot; not comfy on his tricycle, either.'

'Leave it, Stew! Where the hell are our bikes?'

'Hang on and I'll look up the grid reference.'

'The fuzz will find them.'

'Not in this fog.'

'They'll surround the dump.'

'The Prof's bluffing, you driveller. That's what they learn in college, how to bluff their way through. I have thought of signing on for a bit; it's useful know-how. You agree with that, don't you, Rigby?'

'Boy Scouts don't lie; it's in their constitution. But I'm not taking the chance.' Metal clanged; there was an oath.

Stewart said, 'I'd be glad of a helping hand.'

'Listen!'

The fingers on Rigby's arm gripped more tightly. He felt Stewart's body tense. Their ears straining, they picked up the sound of an engine. Labouring, it grew nearer, was joined by a descant of ringing hollow beats.

'Fractured exhaust pipe,' Stewart judged. 'You agree, Rigby? Tubby Weatherill's limping home.'

Col stammered, 'He'll have his dogs. They start sniffing round, fog or no fog, they'll be on to us.'

An elbow ground into Rigby's chest as Stewart levered himself away. 'Sorry to leave you, Sunshine, but I don't fancy being worried by a brace of Alsatians this time of morning. They'll just have to make shift with you.'

Then they had gone, hissing advice to each other on negotiating obstacles and above all, staying cool.

As the clatter of their progress diminished, Rigby considered getting up. Numerous parts of him throbbed but he had no interest in investigating them nor did he particularly wish to explore the damp cut inside the torn trouser leg. What he was most inclined to was sleep.

All he had to do was lay out Gilbert's cycling cape and roll himself in it. There would be no problem with the fog; it would not prevent his dropping off; it was often described as a blanket, so it would be luxuriously warm; and there was no need for him to feel responsible for Henry Watkins, the pseudo hard men had run off, scrambled into the sunset. Watkins could make his own way back to barracks, with or without his tent, because he, Rigby, had had a heavy day. More than that. A day and a half. Half a day followed by a short night followed by another slogging day followed by an evening of spetular . . . spectacular discoveries, followed by a cycle race, a bout of orienteering in a damp dump of a cemetery for every broken-up machine ever invented, and rounded off by a running fight and the threat of a plague of sniffer dogs. And all this early rising, which he assured anyone present he did not plan to make a habit of, and the jumping through one hoop after another that was masquerading as a simple circle on a map, all of this, he had to repeat, was done without a crumb of substantial food passing his parched lips except for a miserable savoury burger and two kindergarten size Cornish pasties, and without the benefit of bennies, cigarettes, or Stupor Juice. So nobody should be surprised he was zombified, a word that went the rounds, he personally had known it start with him then go on to his grandfather, and come back like a boomerang.

He could hear snores and tried to say: 'That's coming on fine, George. Now, still keeping your mouth open, fold your tongue back.' But it was not George snoring and a voice was whispering. It was familiar, but it did not belong to him. A match scratched.

Rigby opened an eye and looked straight into

another one. Round it, the features were concealed by soot. Rigby considered this to be an improvement.

Fifteen

'Mr Livingstone, I presume?' Rigby greeted.

Lips in the soot smiled. 'How did you . . . Why were you here?'

Remembering the reason, he decided instantly that he must not give it to Watkins. He closed his eyes and muttered, 'Good question.'

'I mean, it's well past midnight.'

'I was coming back from Ben's and heard shouts. Left my cycle by the road.'

'At Withy Syke bottom?'

'Could be. I didn't bump into any sign.'

'There isn't one. In any case, the fog would have hidden it.'

'You're on the ball tonight, Watkins.' The danger was passed. 'I can tell you something else I didn't bump into: the Riot Squad. But then I wouldn't, would I?'

'It was a question of expediency. You're not suggesting I go about telling lies? I mean . . .'

Rigby interrupted, 'I was impressed.' Seeing the other's grin, he thought: So I don't mention the true reason Stewart and Col scarpered.

'Do you mind me asking whether you've got a lamp?'

Rigby pulled it out. The casing was badly dented but the rest was undamaged. Its light showed the fog had shrunk and he could see what was scattered around him: stove-in door panels, gritty engines, split radiators, corroded batteries. The remains of a tractor tilted precariously by his side; bending over him were the snapped teeth of a harrow.

'When did the tanks move in?' he murmured.

Not understanding, Watkins informed him, 'The Tank Corps never has exercises round here. I'd appreciate it, Rigby, if I could borrow your lamp. I have to find a car.'

'Have you tired of foot slogging?'

'To be frank, I have, rather.' He accepted the lamp and they searched in its beam. 'I'm looking for a four-door saloon, white.'

'Here's a white one, or was, once. Can you make doors optional?'

'That's no good. It has to be a C registration.'

'You aren't very adventurous, Watkins. Why not go for an H reg. with a complete set of wheels?'

'It's a C I'm after,' he snapped. 'I've hidden the tent in the boot.'

Rigby laughed and went on longer than he wished. I'm losing control through lack of sleep, he explained silently and said, 'I'd benefit from a nap.'

'I hope I'm not holding you up. The car's near a heap of breeze blocks. I know because I took a toss over them.' He did again as he spoke. Not complaining, he searched around.

The lid of the boot was open, the floor rough with dead stalks where grass had grown through. The tent lay on them. It was stained with slurry, grained with grit. 'It's worse than I had hoped.' Watkins' voice had lost its crisp efficiency. There was a long pause, then he managed: 'I don't know what my father will say about this.'

'That ought to be the least of his worries.'

'It's new, never been used before, only for practising, pitching it on the lawn. He timed me. Best I've achieved is four minutes.'

'I like it how it is. More authentic.'

Watkins lifted it out of the boot and held it to his chest. 'Well, I suppose you can say it's been through quite a lot.'

'Your father will appreciate that.'

'I can't tell him what's happened! He would

have seen off those two yobbos with one hand tied behind his back. He sets a high value on fitness. The gym's his second home. That's how he puts it: his second home. You should see the feats he puts himself through.'

For the first time for years Rigby remembered going with his father to Brimham Rocks. Among the bilberries and elegant birches, the great blocks of sandstone were piled in awesome balance, windowed and fluted by winds. They provided a natural adventure playground. And not only for children. Men leapt and scaled until they stood on a high slab, their feet apart, their hands on waists, their chests inflated: proud, invincible. Rigby had been disappointed that Philip had declined to follow their example. But now he was glad. For the men's climb was paltry; the summit gained was a mere seven metres.

Watkins' father would have leapt ahead, though; he would have posed among the supermen and bawled at Henry struggling in his wake.

'They warned me that they would come,' he said, 'and I planned to stand-to all night, but I couldn't. What woke me was the swearing, their flash light's battery had run out. But it had lasted long enough for them to start a fire in this awful place and find where I was encamped. That's not far below here. It was

Stewart that yanked out the pegs. I couldn't stop them striking the tent and I couldn't stop them bringing it here. All I could do was follow them. They were describing how they were going to enjoy setting fire to it.'

'But they didn't, Henry. You prevented them.'

'I couldn't have done if you hadn't been there.'

'I was just stumbling around, hitting out at any opposition.'

'I couldn't work out what was going on and I didn't care. I was trying not to lose track of Col; he had the tent. I heard them talking and went in close. It was mystifying because they were holding someone and seemed to think it was me. So Col had laid the tent down. I saw it when Stewart lit the paper, and I made a grab. Then you shouted and stamped on the flames. The rest is history.' Leaning over the car boot he was silent for a time before pressing down the lid. It grated, then creaked back. Watkins tried again, and gave up. Adjusting his grip on the tent, he said, 'There would be nothing left of this now if you hadn't appeared.'

'That was a chance thing.'

'It seems to me you were acting as decoy.'

'No.' But he was affected by the other's wistful tone and thought: Watkins wants to believe I was deliberately drawing them off. He conceded, 'Although I suppose that's how it turned out. It wasn't possible to go in for any specific planning in that fog.'

It was washing away from them, leaving no trace of its passage but a cold damp in their hair and a gauze of condensation on the car's stained panels.

'Not specific tactics,' Watkins agreed, 'but it's obvious you had an overall strategy.' In this way he chose to be satisfied with Rigby's answer. 'I expect you're keen to get back to your bicycle.'

Which I said was near Withy Syke bottom, Rigby reminded himself, and answered, 'I'm in no hurry.'

'Shall I keep the lamp, pick out the landmarks?'

'I'm very happy for you to waggle it about.'

With these formalities completed, Watkins led Rigby from the dump and down the long bank to Withy Syke. Swinging the lamp, he showed Rigby a shallow gill, clumps of rushes, a broad slick of mud holed by the hooves of cattle.

'It's drier further along and less scruffy,' Watkins told him, admitting the ground's shortcomings. 'I found a sort of shelf, quite ideal for putting up a tent. It can't be far from the lane where your cycle is.'

But when they reached Watkins's solitary camping site, he made no further reference to the bicycle. He found his lantern, lit it and gathered together his scattered equipment: a trekking stove, mess kit, tin opener, cutlery, enamel mug; he made a neat arrangement of vacuum flask, plastic camouflage bottle, water carrier, food containers, first aid tin, spare socks, toilet bag; he brushed soil and grass from the trampled sleeping bag.

'There's not a lot of damage,' he announced. 'The poles are twisted but they can easily be straightened and someone must have stood on the stove because the pan supports are snapped off, but there's no need to upset Dad about it; I can replace them myself. I'm afraid it means a cup of tea or soup is out of the question. Now what else can I offer? Do sit down.' He shook out his towel, arranged it on the ground and rubbed away the print of a boot.

'I know what I have! Coke! It's still in my rucksack. Would you care for a can? Marvellous! I'll join you. Unfortunately, I haven't any tumblers. This coke, may I say,' he said as he rummaged, 'was not in Dad's inventory but I'm sure he wouldn't have objected if I'd suggested it. These cakes weren't on the list, either. Mother baked them late Friday and smuggled them in, although I've got the usual tack – you know, porridge you add water to and wait till it swells, and rissoles and rice to fry. In fact, I couldn't get through all of that. Would you care to sample what's left?' he asked, not slackening in his role of attentive host. 'They're cold, of course. Right! One jumbo helping of rissoles and rice coming up! Sorry? Oh, I thought you said, yes. You aren't generally hungry at this time of morning? I can't say whether I am or not. I'm not awake to find out.'

Watkins's talk continued, helter skelter, demanding no contribution from Rigby, moving from the comfort of his guest to description of the miles he had covered that day, only pausing occasionally to turn his head as if stretching his ear for sounds from the dump. Rigby thought: He's frightened they'll return and all this rabbiting on is to keep me here. Once he began some reassurance but Watkins, affecting nonchalance, broke in with: 'I would never have guessed there would be so many nocturnal animals wandering about Withy Syke. And talking of wandering about, there was an old chap at the stepping stones near Hardisty's Lathe,' and he repeated what he had told Carol.

Rigby said to himself: I ought to be looking for Grandfather, I ought to be searching along this stream; the fog's gone and I've got my cycle lamp. But that illuminated only a few paces ahead of him, not far enough to catch up with a man determined to evade. However, the night was passing. Although its darkness was still held by the bushes and ground, above him there was a hint of sky, a token of morning. He would wait another half hour.

He nodded off, lulled by the monotonous rhythm of Watkins's chat.

A name woke him: Liz Bonniwell.

'Sorry?'

'I'm saying that she mentioned she would be going.'

'Where to?'

'Please don't start pretending again. You know I mean Heather Dale's party.'

'I'd lost the thread.'

The other tutted. 'It sounds as if it's going to be a big do.'

'All the more reason for missing it.'

'I simply can't understand how you could think of declining when one bears in mind the circumstances.'

Rigby was on the point of demanding: What exactly are you suggesting, Watkins? but the other sounded melancholy, left out, so he told him, 'Look, Henry, if you want to go, you'd better have a word with her.'

'You aren't suggesting she could . . .'

'She says she might be able to get you in.'

'That's kind of her. Much appreciated. Thank you for letting me know. I shall certainly get in touch.' He did not whoop with delight, stab the air; nor, to Rigby's relief, did he jump on him and crush him in a sweaty embrace. Instead, he went straight to business. 'It's fancy dress, isn't it? I'm not sure what I can do about that.'

'You'll come up with something.'

'I don't think anything gimmicky, or shall we say "lunatic" would suit. I think I should choose something formal, more serious.'

'What about a funeral director?'

'I don't think that's funny.'

'Exactly. You said you wouldn't go for anything funny.'

There was a pause, then Watkins reproved, 'I believed I could trust your opinion.'

Rigby thought: He's started whining again, and accusing, and at the same time flattering, sycophantic. I should have left him in the dump to fight it out by himself.

Between his feet was the empty can of coke; he took in it a palm and squeezed it to a crumpled wad.

Watkins complained, 'What you don't seem to appreciate is my father would be very upset if I went in for anything flashy.'

'Oh, for heaven's sake! You can have what Carol's borrowed for me. It'll satisfy your father.'

'What's that?'

'A Second World War army uniform.'

'It would be marvellous! Absolutely ideal. I'm very grateful for the offer. Why don't you want to wear it yourself?'

'Spare me. If I go to that party I shall go in civvies, not some antique battledress. That would be sick.'

'It would not. It should make you feel proud.'

'What of? I didn't take part. I wasn't born then, and neither was my mother.' His memory scanned Gilbert's pages. 'I couldn't wear it. I haven't the right.'

For a time the other was intimidated by Rigby's vehemence. Then he said, 'I wouldn't be wearing it to show off, as if I had a stake in what they had done.' He halted, for once unable to find the words. 'Perhaps I ought to ask Liz for her opinion.'

Rigby asked himself: Shall I give him Liz's telephone number? And quickly decided: No. I'll fight for Henry but I'm not carrying flowers for him. He was amused by the fancy.

There were rustles, the first sound of birds. Rigby stood up. 'I'm going.'

'Can you hang on a minute? I've found something. You might like to see it.' Watkins held his lantern over his rucksack, felt in a compartment. 'While I was debating where to erect the tent, I came upon an empty Gaz canister, it must have rolled down from Mr Weatherill's tip. I picked it up, tidying the site, and to my amazement it rattled! There was a hole in it and this was stowed inside.' He handed Rigby a small roll of canvas. 'Have a look. Open it.'

A small cylinder slid into Rigby's palm. It was metal, brass, a cartridge. The round, or shell remained. It had not been fired. Once polished, the surface was dull now, but smooth and unpitted.

'Funny thing to turn up,' Watkins said. 'Different from the usual.' He referred to tubes of coloured card faded by the sun that had fallen from the shot guns of farmers or of men who picked off game.

This cartridge was not filled with small shot for culling rabbits or grouse. The round would bring down a larger target.

'It's for a Walther, the German pistol,' Watkins told him.

. . . it went to Ted soon after and I was the last to have it . . .

Rigby asked, 'How do you know?'

'I walked to the farm for water before Mr Weatherill left. He allowed me to telephone Dad to report my position, so I took the opportunity to describe that.'

Rigby did not listen as Watkins recited the measurements and markings. He was looking at Gilbert's fourth remembrance. It gave off a faint odour of butane from its storage in the gas canister.

'I can't make sense of it,' Watkins grumbled.

'I'm with you there.'

'Do you suppose it could be connected with the old man I came across?'

'That has occurred to me.' His fingers fastened over the shell.

'I don't suppose he could be intending to do someone in, or himself, else he would have hung on to it. Wouldn't he?'

'I'm glad you've pointed that out.'

'Of course, it could have been put here to be safe for future use.'

'The person might have wanted to get rid of it.'

'You could be right,' he agreed, cheered. Then, 'My father said I was to take it home so that he could give it a thorough examination.' His eyes were on Rigby's clenched hand.

'Later, perhaps. I'll let you have the uniform.'

'Thanks. And Rigby – I'm glad you showed up.'

'Think no more about it. I must go.'

'There's a footbridge further down and a path that leads directly to Withy Syke lane.'

'That's handy.' He picked up his lamp and walked by the stream but as soon as he judged he was out of sight he halted, felt inside the cape and, as he had done with the hair, he slipped the cartridge into the pocket Gilbert had made. Then he climbed up the bank, cut through the dump now a ghostly ruin in the tentative light of dawn, collected his cycle and set off for Great Fell.

Sixteen

Once on the lane again, Rigby had not far to ride before reaching the fringe of Great Fell. Stretching for many acres, its slopes were chequered with heather and bilberries and were troughed occasionally by swift cleaving gills. Here and there, strategically positioned, were the neat fortifications of grouse butts.

Since the fell held several small reservoirs, well surfaced tracks had been laid to take maintenance vehicles. Coming to a gate, Rigby saw a notice that warned of shooting during the Season and he thought: Is that the reason Grandfather's final circle is drawn here?

The sky was much lighter now, the ground easing towards it, showing its features. But they were unfamiliar and offered him no guide to beginning a systematic search. When he rode along a made track and reached an intersection, his choice of direction was arbitrary and it obliged him to cycle round a reservoir. There, he found nothing to examine except sluices. What he needed was some viewing point. So he left his bicycle, climbed up a narrow path used by shooters, and aimed for a ridge dark against the horizon. Nearer, it became a broken wall and a few boulders.

Perched on these, he could see only a segment of the land, and that was empty. Whereas he must be visible. He said to himself: If Grandfather were anywhere near, he could see me; and if he can, why doesn't he come? Or will he persist in continuing to hide? Only a few hours were left before Ben told their mother and the police were alerted. Rigby cupped his hands round his mouth, intending to call that Gilbert's respite was almost over but, his lungs full, he felt ridiculous. He did not know what to shout; he could not stand on an open fell shouting for his grandfather like a lost child.

He was caught by a wind; it dragged at his hair and mushroomed the cape. Lower down was a line of butts, solid curves of dry stone walling topped by peaty sods. He strode to them and stood behind a tufty parapet. At his feet was a number of empty cartridges. They were flat, the card soggy with dew. Once they had held small shot. Looking at them, he pushed his fingers into the pocket of the cape and pulled out the brass round and the tress of hair. With them came a strip of paper that he had not seen before.

He smoothed out the folds. One edge of the paper was jagged and the writing on the feint lines was familiar. He had found the piece missing from his grandfather's narrative, the one that had been torn away, torn away after Gilbert had described how he and Rufus had discussed the killings in the farmhouse. When the sergeant had claimed the German's gun: Unfortunately he did not keep it for long. It went to Ted soon after and I was the last to have it. Rufus had said that if he had had the chance he would have let the German shoot himself: 'You should take a man seriously that wants a bullet in his head. If that's the way he wants to go, then he should be allowed.'

Now Rigby read the words on the sliver of paper. I don't regard it as a disgrace to be taken prisoner, like the German did, but I would prefer to be finished off quickly if I hadn't a hope.'

Rigby leant against the wall of the butt and asked himself: Why did Grandfather rip this off? The tear was uneven, indented as if done with effort, jerkily, in distress. Why did he hide it in the pocket of his cape? Could not he bear to read what he had written, Rufe's talk about death?

But these words did not belong only to Gilbert; they belonged to him, too. They were a remembrance of Rufus. So was the hair, it was his true grandfather's; and the round came from the pistol of a man he had killed. Rigby was taken by sadness for this **uncommon man** who had struggled with principles: **Doesn't it bother you? I've killed a prisoner**; who had been appalled that he might shoot because he *wanted* to kill; who had been a competent soldier; who was shocked to have bought Calvados from a girl that had profited from revenge; who was quick tempered, critical, impatient with interruptions of his precarious privacy; who, tender and passionate, spoke the language of flowers; who had, perhaps, foretold his own death: **Green locust tree**, he had said. Affection beyond the grave.

Rigby thought: That's all he can have.

There was the crunch of brittle heather. He turned and Gilbert exclaimed, 'He's not him, I kept telling myself, but my legs wouldn't stop.'

'I'm Rigby, Grandfather.'

'Of course you are. Who says otherwise?'

'Nobody.'

'If they do, I'm not the culprit. I've never muddled you up. But you can't deny the likeness.'

'I don't wish to.'

'For a start, look at today. If I hadn't known what I do, I could have been excused the mistake.'

'What is it you know, Grandfather?'

He evaded the question with: 'That's my cape you've got on. I'd recognise it a mile off. You put your trade mark on it, that smear of paint. Do you remember?'

'Yes.'

'That was a good old day, wasn't it? Harum-scarum you were. Gave me a run for my money.'

Rigby smiled with him. 'You caught me, though.'

'I should have done, me having the longer legs. You pointed that out yourself.'

'You've used them this last couple of days.'

'I have. They feel a bit wonky now.' He was leaning on his spade and his appearance was dreadful. Where dirt had been rubbed from his face the skin was white; a cord of blood trailed from a scratch on his bald crown; round it, the band of hair was flecked with the dust of dry twigs and skeletons of leaves; briars hooked into the turn-ups of his trousers; soil patched the elbows of his jacket; his thin shoes were sodden. The day's light, now thoroughly established, showed a fine mist of steam blurring his shoulders and there was the undeniable odour of damp.

'Shall we go home?' Rigby asked.

'Not before I've finished my commission. The trouble is, what I need seems to be lost.'

'Is this it?' He held out the frayed piece of paper.

'Where was that?'

'In the pocket of your cape.'

'So that's where I put it. I should have guessed, gone back to the gun emplacement.' Then, fierce: 'That cape – you took it away. It shouldn't have been moved. It was keeping something dry.'

'I covered that up.'

Gilbert nodded, satisfied. He took the paper and stated with pretended casualness, 'You'll not have read this.'

'I have.'

'I suppose that's understandable, being there in the pocket. It's not important, a few words someone said to me, one time.'

'I've read the rest, Grandfather.' His fingers were tight over the round from the gun and the lock of hair.

'You have not!'

'I went to your house.' He forced his mind back to when it had started. 'The day before yesterday. I found stuff in the clock. I found your story.'

'That was meant for the eyes of Dr Dixon only. Fenella, she said I was to call her. You shouldn't have taken a look.'

'You're right. But I'm not sorry.'

'How do you mean, you're not sorry? I've never heard anything so brazen, and that's a fact.'

'You've never told me about it. Once I'd begun, I had to finish.'

Flattered, Gilbert confided, 'And there's a lot I didn't put in. Some of the happenings I thought were a bit on the strong side for Fenella. So I didn't give them a mention, or I tore them out. Censorship's the word.'

Rigby thought: He's lying. The pieces he tore out are not descriptions of fighting. One is about how they had rested in the spinney where Rufus thought of Flora and afterwards carried Gilbert's pack. The other piece states how Rufus would prefer to die.

Gilbert read the sentence on the paper, then he rolled it into a tight tube and looked round him, considering the lie of the land. 'I'll be on my way.'

'Grandfather, we've got to get home.'

'Don't you presume to tell me what I must do. That's my business. I expect it's why you're here, to fetch me in. There's been another one, too, on the prowl, looks like a young cadet. He's forever turning up. What's that grin for?'

'You're right; he's forever turning up.'

'He gave me a shock, first time I caught sight of him. I thought the army had been called in.'

'Somebody might be, soon. We've only got till twelve.'

'There's time, then. I can manage.' He did not question Rigby's information, seeming not to be interested. Or perhaps he was too weary for, sitting down, his movements were laboured; it was an effort to ease his shoulders and back into a comfortable position against the butt.

He asked, 'You don't happen to have a sandwich on you, Rigby?'

'I wish I had.'

'A drop of cold tea? Or a pikelet?'

'No. I've eaten all your pikelets. But I've left a note telling you.'

'I expect I'd have noticed they had gone AWOL. We were all given a box of emergency rations for D-Day: compressed porridge in cubes, and the same for milk and tea, sugar lumps, bars of chocolate, boiled sweets. I've mused on those rations a lot, this last couple of days, leaving the house in a hurry and not paying attention to provisions. The box had toilet paper in it, two thin sheets. They had WD − War Department − stamped in one corner. Like the WD they didn't go far. You can imagined how we managed.'

'You didn't put that in your story.'

'I had to keep it decent, Rigby. I didn't want to cause Dr Dixon, Fenella, to have the vapours.'

Encouraged by their laughter, but thinking: I shall regret this, Rigby said, 'It wasn't only that sort of thing you missed out, was it? You missed out a lot more important information than where you relieved yourself.'

Harshly, Gilbert demanded, 'And why shouldn't I? Who are you to say what should go in or stay out? You did wrong to study what I put down. Right from the start I stated it wasn't for any person to read.'

'But I'm not *any person*.' He unclenched his hand, pushed it at Gilbert. The shell rolled in his palm. Freed, the hair leaped up, then was still. 'I'm not *any person*. I'm Rufe's natural grandson.' He was suddenly fearful that he had interpreted the evidence wrongly and pleaded, 'I am, aren't I?'

'You are,' Gilbert whispered.

'These tell me that there is definitely one happening that you did not put in.'

Gilbert did not answer, an old man, exhausted, frail hands knuckling the ground, head bent over these two souvenirs of his war that were polished by the light, undecayed.

Conscious of bullying but desperate lest the

moment slip by, Rigby grated out: 'It is my grandfather's death.'

He saw the other's shoulders flinch. There was a pause, then Gilbert raised his head, stared at him for a moment before looking aside. There was the old, sly slant of his face. 'What makes you think Rufe's dying was any different from the usual run? He was a soldier. He stopped a bullet.'

'It wasn't this bullet though. It hasn't been fired. Why did you hide it on the bank at Withy Syke?'

'You shouldn't ask that question.' But he told him, 'Withy Syke has the look of a certain place, a dirty stream, where we were on stand-by the night the Epsom offensive started. We'd fought in corn and fog. I gave that one a mention.'

'Yes.'

'Rufe was very low. He was young; he confused being good at a job with the liking of it. What I said at the time was the best I could manage. It didn't go far to cheer him.'

'But you tried.'

'Rufe had the Walther in his kit. Little Ted had pushed it on him in Fontenay; he had lost a leg. "You deserve this, Rufe," he said. "I'll just flag down a blood wagon." That was our name for an ambulance. Mind you, by the look of him, he would be finished before

221

one reached him. I knew where the gun was only I couldn't take it without Rufe noticing. I managed to remove the round which went with it, though. You should have left it where it belonged.'

'Grandfather, you aren't saying that Rufus might have shot himself?' He was pleading.

'I'm saying no such thing. He was no coward.'

'So why did you take the bullet?'

'I did it to stop any asking that might come up. Men were going down that fast. Can't you put two and two together — that round in your hand and this paper in mine?'

'I'm frightened to try.'

'And I was. But he wasn't.

'I reckon it would be a fortnight or so after the hand-to-hand fighting in the fog and we'd made no advance, despite there being no let-up. We were practically fought to a stand still. The enemy had brought up more infantry divisions. This day we were south of Tilly, on the flank of the main thrust, with Churchill Crocodiles in support. They were flame-throwing tanks. We were to take some farm buildings and hold a road into Caen. Our company was leading, crossing fields and nervous, there being no sign of the tanks, but we could see grey uniforms moving in the orchard. We held our fire, not wanting to show where we were. Then before we reached the track leading to the farm, we were struck by mortar bombs. That's where Rufe copped it. The mortaring did not stop. Eventually the sergeant – not Sergeant Theaker, of course – got our platoon together and it deployed in a defensive position, meaning it lined up behind a hedge. All twelve men that were left of it. After a while, the order was sent to withdraw. I found my own way back.'

Rigby's expression questioned.

'You don't expect I would leave him alone, do you? I got to him soon as I saw him go down. He was in the hole the shell had made.'

Rigby stared, imagining.

'Don't you look accusing. I did all I could. Anything more was impossible. I have to tell myself that.'

'I'm not accusing you, Grandfather.'

'You – it's like seeing him again, with a few years knocked off. Daphne I never had any trouble with, she favoured Flora, and she's passed it on to Carol. Ben, well, he's got more of Philip in him but not so quiet, more push. Whereas you . . . I'm not talking merely about the colouring; it's all the rest. Rufe did not come out of a regular mould, Rigby, and neither did you. That's made it hard.'

Assuming that Gilbert alluded to the constant

reminder of a dead man whom he had loved, Rigby answered, 'I think I get what you mean.'

'No, you don't. How could you? You weren't there. Every time I look at you, Rigby, it's like I owe you an apology.'

Rigby thought: That sidelong glance, that hopeful expression; and always wanting to be liked, testing my response. But now the old man was shaking, beating his fists on his thighs.

'He was a goner, you see. We both knew it. Even as I held him to me, squatting in that hole, his blood pumped over my chest. But he was young and healthy. Through the grill of his ribs I could see his heart pounding, not giving up. He wheezed, "You've got mud on your hands. You'll be a country lad yet." Then he said, "*Do it, Gilbert. I'd rather arrive in hell like this than in a blood wagon.*" You've read his thought on the matter.' He unrolled the paper.

'Yes.'

'I was aghast. "I can't," I told him. His answer was: "It's an order." He had recently been awarded a stripe.

'I grabbed hold of my rifle, and his, and slung them away.

'"You damn fool," he breathed. "Take the Walther." He lifted a hand, tried to push it inside his battledress and found the blood. His hand flopped down.

'I was near going demented. I managed to extract the pistol. Then I said, "*There's no round.*" That's how I got out of it. "*There's no round,*" I said, when all the time it was lying in my pack.

"Not much to ask." His throat whistled and he gave me a look which told me he guessed what I'd been up to.

'He took a long time to die. I had nothing to stop the pain. Except the bullet. It stayed in my pack. When it was over with him I took a letter out of his kit, it wasn't finished, and the stripe he had never sewn on to his sleeve. I buried the gun. I arranged him as tidy as I could and, last thing, I cut off that lock of hair you're holding. When I came out of the hole things were much the same as they were when I slid into it, apart from there being more dead waiting for collection.

'I don't have any other memory of that day, or of the weeks after. But the final hour with Rufe never left my mind. When you arrived, it was as if he'd come back to tell me he was disappointed. As he had said, it wasn't much to ask, to squeeze the trigger for a dying man. It was his last wish, but even in the middle of all that carnage, I could not do it.

'I let him down, Rigby. I remember that every time I look at you.'

'I'm sorry, Grandfather.'

'It's not a matter for you to apologise for.'

'No. But there are other things.' He thought: I could have been less impatient, less snubbing. More kind.

Gilbert tried to get up and accepted Rigby's hand.

'You said we've only got till noon. What did you mean by that?'

'If I hadn't found you by then, Ben decided he would have to tell Mother. We expected she would report you were missing.'

'So you've kept quiet, the pair of you.'

'Carol, too. She was the one who started me searching.'

'A lovely young woman. Looked nice in that dress she brought, to show it off.'

'Yes. Let's go, get to the track. Ben will be bringing his car.'

'I have to bury this.' He fluttered the slip of paper.

'Why have you chosen here?'

'Because it's where they come shooting, only they call it a sport. It's where these words of Rufe belong.' He was propped against the butt, his hands were on its thatch of turves, picking at the sprouts of heather and the nap of grasses. 'The only thing is, it's a lost cause, hacking through the bracken and such. There's not an inch of broken earth. Different from Normandy.'

'Grandfather, I've got another idea. Instead of burying it, why don't we use this?' He had already pulled the cigarette lighter out of a trouser pocket.

Gilbert peered at it. 'I must have left that at a house a day or two back. There had once been an abbey nearby.'

'Yes.'

'It's a certain make. Do you know what we gave its name to?'

'Yes.'

'You've been learning a lot, these last days.'

'That's right.' He held the lighter in the shelter of the wall and pressed down with a thumb. Immediately a flame shot up. Then, almost panting because the gamble was so big, he managed: 'After all these years I reckon that Rufe would wish you to do away with what he asked of you.' The flame jumped.

For a long time his grandfather regarded it, then his eyes went to Rigby. They lingered over his hair, his face, took in the cape, then examined the wide shoulders and the feet firm on the spent tubes of cartridges. And Rigby knew that it was not he that Gilbert saw.

He held his breath.

'So that is your opinion?' Gilbert whispered. 'Can I take it as a truth?'

Rigby nodded.

Gilbert straightened the paper and slowly brought it to the light. Together he and Rigby watched the words curl, bow to the flame's heat, become crisp and darken until they floated down. Within the walls of the grouse butt they came to rest, a small drift of soft, forgiving ash.

FOUNDLING

June Oldham

It is the future.

Ren is alone, living rough on the bleak moors. She meets Brocket, a boy born to the wilderness, Lil, brave and untamed, Hilary, strange and mysterious, and Found, a baby, but the most important one of all . . .

Together they must survive dangers – hostile patrolmen, an unknown pursuer, the perils of the moors, and another greater than any of these.

SMOKE TRAIL

June Oldham

Living with her mother and grandmother, Cora longs for her absent father. She grows convinced that he, too, wishes them to meet.

But the search for him is like tracing a smoke trail hiding a smouldering, hidden fire. It stirs old stories, disturbs memories in Cora's family and present Cora with a shocking choice . . .

UNDERCURRENTS

June Oldham

Fergal and his mother are nursing an old lady while her family is away. It's an isolated farm in Yorkshire; a hot, rainless summer. In the nearby reservoir the water is falling . . .

Then Fergal meets the girl, Alex, who watches the drying reservoir, waiting. Just as the old lady and everyone in the valley watches the waters fall. Seeing the spire in the drowned village reach upwards . . .

Feeling old memories rise . . .

And Fergal's own memories flow in those undercurrents – memories that somehow, finally, with Alex, he too must face . . .

ESCAPE

June Oldham

Are there some secrets that can't be told?

Magdalen has finished school and is about to leave home. Freedom at last, final and total escape.

But her father has other plans.

So she runs away, away from him and their terrible secret. With her goes Greg, a stranger, and gradually through him the power of the secret is broken.

Together they conquer Magdalen's past and she faces the future with hope.

A deeply moving story about a girl escaping from incest.

THE RAVEN WAITS

June Oldham

Then the night of waiting began to close around Hrethric. The darkness, fanged with ice, bit through his covering of fur; it tightened over his head; creatures spawned in its breath and crawled over his skin; and its rancid fumes entered his mouth and lodged like a swab in his throat. He was stifled; his arms were pinned to his sides; his mind spun . . .

The Scylding kingdom has been gripped by terror for twelve long years. Nightly visitations from the monster, Grendel, have seen its mightiest warriors devoured, its people crippled, and its king immobilised by guilt and grief.

The king's son, Hrethric, can see no end to the devastation. But the coming of Beowulf, the Great hero, brings hope . . .